Her Amish Heart

Samantha Bayarr

Her Amish Heart

Copyright © Samantha Bayarr 2019

Scripture quotations are from New King James Version of the Bible.

GLOSSARY

ach: oh

aenti: aunt

boppli: baby

brudder: brother

danki: thank you

dat: father, dad

dawdi: grandfather

dochder: daughter

Englisher: a person who is not Amish

Fraa: wife

Frau: married woman

Freinden: friends

Gude mariye: good morning

gut: good

haus: house

jah: yes

kaffi: coffee

kapp: prayer cap

kinner: children

kume: come

mei: my

mamm: mom, mother

narrish: crazy, foolish

naerfich: nervous

onkel: uncle

Ordnung: rules of the Amish faith

Schweschder: sister

Wilkum: welcome

A NOTE FROM THE AUTHOR

While this story is set against the real backdrop of an Amish community, the characters and the town are fictional. There is no intended resemblance between the characters and community in this story and any real members of the Amish or communities. As with any work of fiction, I've taken license in some areas of research as a means of creating the necessary circumstances for my characters and the community in which they live. My research and experience with the Amish are quite knowledgeable; however, it would be impossible to be entirely accurate in details and description since every community differs, and I have not lived near enough the Amish community for several years to know pertinent and current details. Therefore, any inaccuracies in the Amish lifestyle and their community portrayed in this book are due to fictional license as the author.

Thank you for being such a loyal reader.

TABLE OF CONTENTS

CHAPTER ONE

CHAPTER TWO

CHAPTER THREE

CHAPTER FOUR

CHAPTER FIVE

CHAPTER SIX

CHAPTER SEVEN

CHAPTER EIGHT

CHAPTER NINE

CHAPTER TEN

CHAPTER ELEVEN

CHAPTER TWELVE

CHAPTER THIRTEEN

CHAPTER FOURTEEN

CHAPTER FIFTEEN

Special Offers

CHAPTER ONE

SOPHIE Webber planted her hands on her hips defiantly and looked her father straight in the eye as if to stand her ground. "I can't go an entire summer without my cellphone or my computer," she argued. "How will I talk to my friends?"

"You can send them a letter!" her father said.

"You mean like—in the mail?" she squealed. "I only have their phone numbers and email addresses. They'd laugh at me if I sent them a letter in the mail."

Her father scowled at her from around his newspaper. "If they'd laugh at you over something that simple, then you can't really count them as very good friends, can you?"

Tears welled up in Sophie's eyes as she sat in the chair across from him at the breakfast table. "But Dad! You said all I had to do was finish college to get my trust fund; why are you putting another condition on it when I already did as you asked me to do?"

"You're twenty-five years old, and that's too old to argue with me like a child," he reprimanded her. "You might have finished college, but there isn't much you can do with a Liberal Arts Degree, and I'm not convinced you've grown up. Spending the summer helping someone other than yourself will help you grow up, and this is the best way; to go away and learn about a slower way of life."

"More like the nineteenth century!" Sophie complained. "The Amish are so slow; they're a backward society. If you want me to experience other cultures, why do I have to do that in an Amish community? You could send me to Hawaii instead; I could learn a lot from the natives there!"

Hugh Webber folded his newspaper with a snap and glared at his daughter. Mrs. Hildebrand, their cook, placed a plate of poached eggs and toast in front of him and he set the newspaper on the table. He took a sip from the coffee the woman refilled for him before he resumed their conversation.

"I've made up my mind," Hugh said with a firmness his daughter didn't care for. "I should have done this years ago—long before you became so spoiled. You need to learn a few life-lessons. Things I can't teach you. I've spoiled you with a cook and a housekeeper, and you don't even know how to boil water or sew on a button. The Amish can teach you those things better than anyone, and it won't cost me like your expensive, private school, and the countless musical lessons, riding lessons, and dance lessons you gave up on too easily."

Sophie pushed back the bowl of fresh fruit in front of her and folded her arms over her middle. "I don't need to know how to sew a button," she said. "I can just buy a new blouse!"

Hugh put down his forkful of eggs and wagged his finger at his daughter. "That's exactly the mentality that caused me to finally make this decision; you don't know the value of hard work. You don't even understand the concept of how to survive without servants and cooks."

"I just finished college: that's hard work!" she protested. "And I had to go without a cook and a housekeeper the whole time I was there."

He pursed his lips and scowled. "That doesn't count; you ate takeout the entire time, and if I remember, your roommate had her housekeeper come in and clean your dorm once a week! There's a whole world out there you know nothing about, Sophie. You need to mature so you don't end up spending your trust fund on frivolous things that will leave you bankrupt in less than a year. Taking this job is the *only* way you're getting access to your trust fund—and only *after* the summer is over. If your mother was alive, she'd…" his voice trailed off.

Sophie leaned forward, eager for him to finish his sentence. "She'd what, Dad?"

He looked away without answering her.

Silence fell between them, and her father picked up his newspaper and held it in front of his face. It was what he did every time he *almost* spoke of her mother. It had been that way all her life, and Sophie couldn't understand why he wouldn't talk about her. She knew the pain in his eyes and his voice when he tried to talk about her. Sophie wished she could remember more about her mother than the few foggy memories that didn't amount to much, and she couldn't understand her father's reluctance to share things about her. She knew her father still missed her mother, but it was tough for Sophie to miss a mother she didn't remember having.

She reached over and touched her father's arm lightly; she hated the silence between them. "Tell me how you found the job for me," she almost begged. It wasn't what she wanted to talk about, but she couldn't stand it when he shut her out.

He lowered his newspaper, letting it rest across his plate. "I was taking a drive out in the country—we used to live on a farm when you were little; do you remember that?"

Sophie picked at the blueberry muffin in front of her and shrugged her shoulders. "Not really; didn't we move here when I was five?"

Hugh gave a curt nod, letting her know not to take the conversation any further toward talk of her mother. Through bits and pieces of conversations over the years, she'd learned they'd lived on a farm, but they'd moved to the city after her mother's funeral. She was only five years old at the time, and she had only a vague hint of a memory of the funeral.

"I met an Amish man while I was out there looking around; his name is Simon Yoder," her father said.

Sophie resisted the urge to roll her eyes; weren't all Amish people named *Yoder?*

"He's a nice fellow—a widower, and his mother recently suffered a mild stroke, and he needs help while she recovers because she can't take care of his two young daughters until she gets some physical therapy."

"Why would he want *me* to take care of his daughters?" Sophie asked. "I don't know anything about kids! And who does the cooking and cleaning?"

Hugh cleared his throat. "*You* will."

"Me?" she squealed. "I don't know how to cook anything!"

"You'll learn," he said with a calm reassurance she wasn't buying.

Sophie tossed her napkin on her plate. "It would take months of lessons from the finest chefs to teach me how to boil water!"

"Simon has assured me his mother can teach you."

"How is she supposed to teach me when she can't take care of the kids?"

Hugh gave his paper a snap to crease the middle and folded it once more, placing it next to his plate. Sophie gulped; experience warned her he was losing his patience with her and she'd be doing herself a favor if she closed her mouth and listened or this *punishment* was only going to get worse.

"The woman can still talk," her father said. "She has some paralysis on one side and can't walk very well, and she can't lift anything. But she still has all her faculties, and she will be there to instruct you on everything."

"I don't want her breathing down my neck all day watching everything I do!" Sophie said. "Oh, Dad, this is going to be the worst summer of my life—worse than the time you sent me to summer camp with all those dirty kids!"

"Those kids weren't dirty—they were *normal* kids who were underprivileged and didn't have designer clothes to wear the way you do," he said firmly.

"Like the Amish!" she said with an eye-roll. "Don't they sew their clothes out of flour sacks or something?"

Her father let out a low growling sigh. It was time for her to be quiet.

"If I recall, you had fun at that camp and didn't even want to come home at the end of the two weeks!" Hugh said. "Who knows, you might feel the same way about living among the Amish for a few months."

"Not likely!" she mumbled.

Sophie searched through her walk-in closet full of designer clothes, mourning the loss of them. She would miss them and her collection of designer shoes and purses her father ordered her to leave behind while she packed for her summer job.

This isn't going to be just a job; it's going to be a punishment, too!

His instructions had been simple enough; either she takes the job at the Amish farm, or she could kiss her trust fund goodbye. Why had he thought to choose the worst possible job for her? He'd given her a lecture about teaching her life lessons that she didn't learn while she was away at school, *blah-blah-blah.* She'd stopped listening to him after he informed her she had to leave her cell phone and laptop behind. The final blow had come when he'd presented her with the awful *uniform* she was to wear. It seemed that the Amish family *loaned* her a used dress and apron to wear, and a pair of black shoes she wouldn't be caught dead in. Even though the housekeeper had laundered the dress for her, the dress was still dingy and brown—like a potato sack—and it smelled like a barn!

Her father had seemed a little harsh when he'd explained that if she wanted more than one dress, she had to learn to sew it herself. She couldn't imagine trying to sew a dress; of course, the dress they'd given her was quite primitive. She supposed if she had to, she could trace around the material and cut out a pattern from that. She doubted they used patterns like the rest of the world.

Sophie let out a discouraging sigh; everything she was allowed to take with her didn't even fill a backpack.

She slumped down on the edge of her bed; she was grateful all her friends would be vacationing in nice places over the summer and wouldn't really have time for her anyway. She was certainly jealous of them, but at least she wouldn't be embarrassed by having to explain her plans to her friends.

Reclining onto her down feather comforter, she wished she could smuggle it into her backpack—that and her pillows.

They'll probably make me sleep in the barn, and I'll smell like cows and pigs all day!

Then a thought occurred to her; Kyle was the only person she knew who wasn't going away for the summer, and that was because he worked at his father's used-car lot. She hated to ask him for a favor because she was trying to cut ties with him, but she needed someone to bail her out in case things weren't going well. With no communication with the outside world, she needed an out—just in case.

She dialed Kyle's number, and he picked up on the first ring.

"Hey, I was just getting ready to call you to see if you wanted to go to the beach with me for the weekend," he said. "My buddies rented a condo, and they want me to go in with them, but you know I never have any money."

Sophie sighed; he was always asking her for money this way—without really asking her. It annoyed her that he thought she was an ATM or something.

"How much do you need?" she asked sarcastically.

"I don't want you to pay," he said, stumbling over his words. "I wanted you to go with me—you know—as my guest."

"You know I won't go anywhere with you unless I could have my own room," she said.

"When are you going to stop teasing me and stop saving yourself for marriage?"

Sophie bit her bottom lip to keep from calling him a jerk; she called him because she needed his help, and arguing with him and calling him names would not get her anywhere.

"I can't go; my dad is making me take a summer job!"

"Doing what?" he asked.

She blew out a breath before answering, bracing herself for him to tease her.

"A nanny to some Amish kids."

He chuckled. "Are you serious?"

She sighed again. "Yes!"

He let out another chuckle. "Oh wow; that's rough!"

"I need someone to help me out of it in case I have to bail," she explained. "Will you help me?"

He laughed some more until it dawned on him that she needed his help.

"Okay, but it's going to cost you!"

CHAPTER TWO

After the humiliation of handing over her cell phone and laptop to her father, Sophie let herself into the passenger side of her father's car. She'd said a sad goodbye to her car too; he had forbidden her to drive herself to her new *job*. She was completely cut off until she passed his little test. After that, she'd be a free woman and could use her trust fund any way she pleased. Until then, she was angry with him and wasn't even sure she wanted to talk to him.

She stared out the window while the radio played classical jazz; her father knew it calmed her, but now it served to fill the quiet void between them. She squirmed in her seat a little and adjusted her seatbelt; this was almost as bad as riding in an elevator full of strangers while everyone ignored each other except to make pointless small-talk. Only, she and her father weren't even making small-talk. They were simply ignoring each other—or maybe it was just her. She only knew it was irritating her.

An hour into the trip, they pulled off the highway onto a rural road; how far had he driven to find this Amish farm? Was there a specific destination he'd had in mind the day he'd come across the Yoder place? If so, did it have anything to do with where they had lived? She'd asked him a time or two over the years, but she'd given up when he refused to discuss anything to do with their farm. Now that she was being forced to take the job as nanny to the Yoder children, she was curious why he was suddenly willing to hint around about the subject. But as always, he clammed up as soon as her prying went too far.

Sophie watched the landscape whizzing by, boredom overtaking her to the point she wished she could get out and walk. Ignoring her mix of emotions, she mindlessly thought about the inhabitants of the occasional farmhouse they passed and wondered if she was happy as a child when they lived on a farm. Would she find anything about farm life familiar to her when she arrived on the Yoder farm, or would it be awkward and difficult?

Sophie hugged her sides and leaned against the window, ignoring the uneasiness in her gut. She shouldn't have eaten breakfast before they left; coffee would have been enough, and it wouldn't have given her heartburn. She reached for her bottle of water in the center console and took a large sip.

Gulping it down with a whip of her head toward the passing farm, she nearly dropped the water bottle in her lap.

"Stop the car!" she squealed, gripping her father's arm.

"What's wrong?"

She didn't answer; her neck was craned behind her as she watched out the back window.

Hugh slowed down and pulled over onto the grassy shoulder of the country road, and Sophie jumped out and ran back toward the farm they'd passed. She slowed her pace, walking slowly through the tall grass, ignoring her father's voice calling after her. Instead, she focused her gaze on the jerky movement of the windmill. It squeaked with every turn and shifted from side to side, the smallest breeze animating it. She stopped in her tracks, the high grass waving and tickling against her bare calves.

What was it about that windmill that had her so mesmerized?

"Mamma!" She whispered.

A glimpse of her mother rushed over her, a flutter of contentment rising from her heart. She tried to hold onto the memory, but it left her just as swiftly as it filled her. Her heart raced as if she was still running. That was the strongest memory she'd ever had of her mother. Why couldn't she ever hold onto the memories for more than a passing moment? Bliss turned to gloom within seconds.

Her throat constricted; for the first time in her life, she was feeling something other than indifference about her mother. By the time her father caught up with her, a single tear had rolled down her cheek. She quickly swiped at it before turning around; the memory was gone, and she couldn't get it back.

She walked past her father toward the car with him on her heels demanding an explanation from her. Even if she could give him one, she wouldn't. He would shut her down and refuse to answer the myriad of questions that had plagued her since she'd learned to talk. She stomped her feet and pursed her lips; it wasn't fair for him to keep her mother from her.

When she reached the car, she collapsed onto the passenger's seat and slammed her door. When her father got in, she turned her head away and bit her bottom lip to keep the tears stinging the backs of her eyes from giving away what she was feeling. If he knew, he'd ask her what was wrong and then she'd have to tell him and put up with him clamming up about the subject.

No thanks!

He sat next to her in silence, and she could feel his eyes on her; he wanted an explanation from her, but she would not give him one no matter what.

"I wish you'd tell me what that was all about," he said.

"You wouldn't understand," she mumbled.

After a few minutes, he started the car and pulled back onto the asphalt, ribbons of road still ahead of them.

"Will you forgive me?" he asked, breaking the silence.

Her jaw clenched, and she let her head drop against the window.

"For what?" she mumbled. "Exiling me to Amish country, or for cutting me off?"

"For spoiling you," he said gently. "I made a promise to your mother…"

His voice trailed off, but she hadn't missed the crack in his voice when he mentioned her mother. She knew how much pain he was still in even after twenty years had elapsed since her mother had passed away. She'd just experienced a hint of what that loss felt like and could no more process her feelings about that than she could relate to her father's pain. Though she couldn't remember enough to feel strongly about her mother, it broke her heart that she'd been without her for her whole life. If she'd remembered more than the scant recollection of the woman, she might have a better understanding of what she should be feeling, but it was hard to miss something she didn't remember having.

What could she say now? Was her heart so hardened that she had lost compassion for her father? No! She turned around in her seat and placed a hand on his and gave it a gentle squeeze.

"When you come home," he said. "We'll talk, and I'll answer all your questions;

promise me you'll give this job your best and keep an open mind about this."

She nodded reluctantly. "I'll try."

He slowed down the car and turned into a long driveway that led to a white clapboard farmhouse with black shutters. Sophie felt a familiarity about the place, but she kept it to herself; most of the farms they'd passed on the way over had the same general look about them. She stared at the house, her heart taking a faster pace. Her mouth felt dry, and her legs felt wobbly as she tried to get out of the car. She coughed when she breathed in deeply; how did people live with the animal smell without losing their breakfast every day?

She clamped a hand over her nose and mouth and groaned. Her father breathed in deeply and smiled.

"That's fresh air you're smelling!" he said cheerfully.

She shook her head and frowned, her eyes watering. "I think that's cow manure!"

She stood there for a few minutes, letting her gaze roll over the property. The wraparound porch boasted a hanging swing at both ends. All along the front, hydrangeas with huge clusters of white, lavender, and pink blooms drew her toward them. She bent to push her nose in them, disappointment filling her at their lack of scent. From the look of them, she would think they would smell better than roses, but strangely, their hint of a scent was familiar to her.

She turned around and glanced at her father. "Do we know the people who live here? The house seems a little familiar."

"I've only met them once, and you've never met them," he answered, looking off toward the barn.

There was something he was keeping from her, and it made her stomach clench. She decided not to push him; it wasn't worth it. She was about to have to tell him goodbye for three entire months, and it was best if she tried to part on good terms. He irritated her, but she adored him; he'd always been a good father. Truthfully, this was really the only thing he'd ever asked her to do for him with such sincerity. Sure, he'd demanded that she finish college, but that didn't seem to mean as much to him as this, and she wondered why.

Was there really a lesson she was to learn before the summer was over? Whatever it was, she was betting it would be a hard lesson.

Two little girls came rambling out the door and stopped before descending the stairs of the porch when they saw Sophie. They were dressed in the same light blue dresses with white aprons, and their blond hair was twisted up and pinned behind their heads. Their bare feet were filthy, and their bright blue eyes stared at her. If not for one being a head taller than the other, she would have guessed they were twins.

"Hello," Sophie said timidly.

They ran back into the house.

Sophie turned around and shrugged at her father. "What did I do? Was I not supposed to talk to them?"

Hugh pointed to the front of the house where a man walked out with the little girls who stood close to him.

"It looks like they went inside to get their father."

"Mr. Yoder," her father said as he walked up to greet the man.

Sophie's breath hitched when he removed his hat revealing dark blonde hair. He was extremely handsome—not at all the way she'd pictured him. She'd expected an older man with a thick, scraggly beard hanging from his chin, but he was young and clean-shaven. She'd expected him to be dirty and unkempt in every way, but he was wearing a crisp blue dress shirt and black pants with suspenders. His black hat was sporty, and she thought it suited him. Had he gotten dressed up for their visit?

Sophie didn't know what to think of Mr. Yoder; she stood back and let her father converse with him. She couldn't take her eyes off him; was her father *really* going to let her live with this handsome man for three whole months? How was she going to get through the summer without giving away her attraction to him?

Her father turned around and beckoned her up to the porch. "This is Simon Yoder and his two daughters, Katie and Ellie."

Sophie extended a hand to Simon, not knowing how to greet him, but he didn't take her hand or shake it. She lowered it when he cast his eyes downward. He wouldn't even look at her! How was she going to live in this man's house if he wouldn't look at her or speak to her? Was that the Amish way?

She could only guess that as a woman she was not allowed to address him as a man.

Simon nodded curtly. "The *kinner* will take you in the *haus* to meet *mei mudder* and get you settled." Then he excused himself to Hugh and walked away.

Sophie hadn't really understood a word he'd said and wanted to jump back in the car and demand her father take her home immediately.

She leaned in toward her father and whispered while the little girls stood there and stared at her. "I can't stay here; that man doesn't want me here."

Hugh patted her arm. "He's a grieving widower; it might take him a little time to warm up to you."

The younger of the two girls approached her and tugged on her arm. Sophie looked down into her soulful eyes and smiled.

She smiled back and studied Sophie for a minute. "You look like *mei mamm!*"

Sophie turned to her dad and flashed him a look to help her out; she had no idea how to respond to such a comment.

"I have to go," her father said abruptly.

He hugged her rigid frame, and she whispered in his ear. "Dad, you can't leave me here like this—without an explanation!"

"You need to stay here," he reassured her. "Your mother would be proud."

Sophie pulled away from him and looked him in the eye. "She would? Why?"

"Stay here, and we'll talk when the summer is over," he said, his misty eyes clouding up with remorse.

Sophie stepped away from her father; her backpack slung over one shoulder; she was upset and unable to keep from feeling unwanted.

CHAPTER THREE

Sophie stood there biting back tears as she watched her father back out of the Yoder's driveway. Was her trust fund worth all of this? Living with a man and his mother and two kids—living with strangers? All thoughts of Simon being handsome had gone out the window the minute he snubbed her just now. She was nothing more than a nanny, and the two of them would likely not even be so much as *friends*. She could never be friends with such a rude person.

Everything in her wanted to start walking back toward town, but she couldn't even be sure there was a *town* for miles and miles. They hadn't passed anything but long stretches of farms for more than an hour after leaving the highway. She was lost out in the middle of nowhere, and she was stuck until her father came to get her in three long months.

She immediately thought of the track phone Kyle had talked her into getting last night; it would be her safety net if she needed it. But where would she stay until the summer was over so she could collect her trust fund? And how would she keep him from knowing she wasn't here when he came back for her? She needed to think past her nervous stomach and a million thoughts were crowding her mind right now.

Meanwhile, Simon Yoder's daughters stared at her, and she couldn't think.

Why were they so quiet?

She paced back and forth on the front lawn, biting her bottom lip; she couldn't look at the girls right now. It was nerve-wracking enough that they wouldn't stop watching her. Then she looked up and saw an old woman staring at her from the front window. She stopped pacing; her mouth went dry, and she felt faint in the hot sun. Her legs suddenly felt like jelly; why was she still here? Shouldn't she have walked away by now? She pulled in a deep breath and looked at the girls finally, and her heart skipped a beat; they needed her, and she *had* to stay.

"Would you like to sit on the porch with us to get out of the hot sun?" the older girl asked.

Sophie nodded and followed them to the porch swing. It was good to be in the shade. Wiping the sweat from her brow, she watched the two of them climb up on the swing. She sat in one of the rockers that looked homemade.

"Which one of you is Ellie, and which one is Katie?" she asked them.

They each pointed to themselves.

Sophie blew out a breath. "Let me try that again; which one is Ellie?"

The oldest one pointed to herself, and the younger one pointed to her older sister. At least now she knew which one was which.

She leaned down to the younger one. "That means you must be Katie."

The young girl nodded.

She knew from her father's vague description of the family that the girls were five and seven—about the same age she was when she lost her mother. He'd told her that their mother had passed away a year ago, but these girls seemed well-adjusted. Had she been? All she could remember was a lot of crying—crying that seemed to stretch on for years, though she was certain it hadn't been that long.

Sophie could feel the eyes of the old woman on her from the moment she sat in the chair. Did she think Sophie was rude for not coming inside? The truth was, she wasn't ready to go inside; she couldn't even be sure she was going to stay. Yes, the girls needed her, but did she need them? Maybe, but only so she could get her trust fund. She let out a sigh as she sat there in silence realizing she suddenly sounded extremely selfish. Here were these two little girls who had no mother and all she could think about was her money. She knew how it felt not to have a mother; she didn't wish that void on anyone, especially not a couple of innocent children who didn't ask for such a tragedy any more than she had.

"What do you do during the day?" she asked them, hoping to end the silence that tore at her gut.

"We do chores and clean the *haus,*" the older one said.

Sophie made a face and then corrected it by forcing a smile. "Chores?"

"We feed the chickens and get the eggs."

The younger one's face lit up. "Would you like to see the chickens?"

Sophie shrugged. She didn't want to, but the girl was so eager to show her, how could she possibly say no. "Okay."

They each stood up and walked down the porch steps, and she followed them. When they got around the side yard where the barn was, Katie slipped her hand in Sophie's, and it shocked her. She pulled on Sophie to get her to follow her to a little barn-like structure she could only assume was where the chickens were.

In a fenced-in area behind the shed, chickens clucked and pecked at the ground. She'd never seen a chicken up-close, and she was grateful they were penned in.

Katie tugged on her arm. "Do you want to pet them?"

Sophie shook her head, trying to keep her knees from shaking. Staying outside the fence was close enough for her comfort. Wearing the dress uniform her father had given her, she feared the animals pecking at her ankles and making her bleed.

"You don't have to be scared," Ellie said to her.

Sophie jutted out her chin. "I'm not afraid!" she fibbed. "I just think they should get to know me first before I go disturbing them, that's all."

The girls giggled. "They won't peck at you, but they might flap their wings. *Dat* clips them so they can't fly away."

Sophie laughed. "I didn't know chickens could fly!"

"They will roost in the trees if you don't clip the wings," Ellie said. "Then we would have to climb the tree to get the eggs, or they would fall in the grass and break. Penny—the big one," she said, pointing to the red hen. "She used to fly up in the tree, and she'd drop her eggs all the time."

For two shy little girls, they were suddenly very talkative and very informative.

"Where do you get the eggs now?"

Ellie pointed to the shed door. "We get them from the nesting boxes in the chicken coop. Do you want to see?"

Her heart sped up but how could she say no to them? If they were brave enough to get near the chickens, she should be; she was bigger and could run faster if she needed to!

Ellie opened the door, and the two girls went inside the coop. Sophie stood back a little to make sure it was safe before following them. With skylights on the roof, it was light inside, and she could see boxed off sections against the walls in stacks. Several chickens rested in the boxes and Katie walked right up to one and stuck her hand underneath the white hen, and it didn't even flinch. She pulled out a brown egg and showed it off to Sophie with a smile.

Sophie giggled. "That seemed easy enough."

"You try it!" Katie urged her.

Sophie shook her head. "Maybe later; I'm a stranger to the chickens, and they might have to get to know me first like I said. I don't want to upset them."

"It's alright," Ellie assured her. "We'll be right here."

Sophie inched her way toward one of the white hens and extended a shaky hand toward the box, aware that the chicken was staring right at her. She held her breath and moved her hand slowly toward the box and rested it near the chicken.

I can't let the girls or the chicken know how scared I am!

She moved slowly—cautiously, trying not to disturb the animal. Her hand made contact with the feathers and continued to move until she could feel the straw on the side of the nest. Pushing her hand further down, she felt around carefully, ever aware that the chicken was now resting on her hand. She felt an egg and grabbed for it, pulling it out faster than she'd pushed her hand in there, causing the chicken to squawk and flap it's wings.

Sophie squealed and dropped the egg on the straw-covered floor and backed up while the girls giggled and pointed at her.

"I don't want to do that again!" Sophie said.

"You'll get used to it," Ellie said.

No, I won't!

"Dat said you'll be helping us with the chores so you will get used to getting the eggs in a couple of days or so. I promise."

Their father told them she was going to help with the chores too? She thought she was only here to babysit and help them with cooking dinner—like doing the heavy stuff. What had she agreed to? Her father hadn't said anything about doing chores like getting eggs from these crazy chickens!

"What else did your dad say I'd be helping with?" She was almost afraid to ask.

"He said you were going to help with the wash and hanging clothes on the line because I have to stand on a chair, and Katie has to hand me the clothes from the basket."

"Why do you do so much?"

Ellie shrugged. "We are the only ones who can do it."

"What about your dad?"

"He takes care of the animals in the barn, and he makes buggies."

Sophie bit her bottom lip to keep from laughing. "Buggies?"

Ellie nodded. "To ride into town and to church. *Dat* makes the buggies for everyone. The Bishop lets him sell them in the community even though we don't go to church with them."

Sophie didn't know what to think about that. Her father had told her they have a leader in their community who was the Bishop, but for some reason, she thought she already knew that. She assumed she'd heard it somewhere, but she'd also done some research on the Amish on her computer before her father had taken it away from her. She'd learned how hard they work—even the children. It seemed strange to her that the family would all work together so hard just to live their everyday lives. They all pitched in and helped each other build houses and barns too. The women cooked and baked and cleaned the house—all without electricity.

"Do you have electricity in the house?" She *had* to ask.

"*Dat* was going to put some in, but we use gas for the stove and for heat."

"Do you have air conditioning?"

Ellie shrugged. "What's that?"

Sophie knew it was a long-shot, but she *had* to ask. She'd read that they didn't have such things and most of them didn't even have a furnace. They used fireplaces and wood stoves to keep their houses warm in the winter. She was grateful that she was here over the summer instead of winter. She'd rather be too warm than too cold any day.

"Never mind," Sophie said. "Maybe we should go in now so I can meet your grandmother; she's probably wondering why we haven't come in yet."

Katie smiled. "You're going to like *Mammi.*"

"Is that what you call your grandmother?"

Ellie smiled and nodded. "You talk like an *Englisher.*"

"I'm sorry; it will probably take me a little while to learn your words. Let's go inside so I can meet your *mammi.*"

The girls giggled, but Sophie forced a smile to cover over her nervousness. Conversing with the girls was easy, but the thought of being under the watchful eye of Simon's mother was enough to make her lose her breakfast.

I sure hope she likes me! Sophie worried as she followed the girls in through the back door of the house.

CHAPTER FOUR

Simon walked out to the barn, his insides churning like a fresh batch of butter. The minute he laid eyes on Sophie, he knew what Hugh Webber had told him was true. If he'd known that Hugh's daughter would remind him so much of his Becca, he never would have agreed to have her here. How was he going to get through an entire summer with her in his house and having to see her every day without it crushing his heart? His immediate thought was to send her away, but Hugh Webber had given him the money already to take her in, and it had paid the back taxes on his farm. He'd neglected his work since Becca had passed away and had let his finances dwindle to the point he needed the money. He wasn't about to ask the Bishop for help after he'd denounced the church and refused to take the baptism. He wanted to make the move to being Mennonite. He still believed in the humble ways of the Amish, but he could not in good conscience, commit to the church. The Bishop had agreed not to shun Becca after they were married, but some in the community did. Simon thought it was because he hoped to win him over and change his mind, but he never did. He enjoyed having family and friends in the community, but he didn't believe as they did. He was more of a free-thinker, and they were too strict, and for that reason, he could never go to them for help paying his back taxes.

Lord, give me the strength to give this young woman the chance to explore her place in this community while she's here; help me not to get in the way of what you have planned for her life.

He blew out a breath and grabbed a pitchfork to muck out the stalls. Hard work would keep his mind off the beautiful Sophie, wouldn't it? Perhaps after he'd worn himself out, he would have enough guts to go inside and welcome the young woman properly. He had to go inside sooner or later; the meal would be ready, and he'd have to take his things from his room and take them out to the *dawdi haus*. He chided himself for not doing that before she arrived. Now, he would feel awkward doing that in front of her. It was possible he could slip into the house unnoticed and clear out his things while she was preoccupied with his mother and daughters.

What had he gotten himself into? He was thankful his parents had built a *dawdi haus* the first year after they'd purchased the home. The inside of the house was so quaint that they hadn't done any renovations and he wondered if Sophie would find it familiar.

Midnight whinnied and bobbed his head through the open barn window from the corral;

he was ready to go back to his stall and eat his oats and fruit, and Simon was taking his time with cleaning the gelding's stall.

Lord, help me to keep mei mind on task, and keep it off the young woman named Sophie. Give me the strength to resist the temptation she presents. Forgive me for being attracted to her. I know you don't see it as betraying Becca's memory, but I still do. I know everything happens for a reason, and I pray you will reveal your reason for her being here—to her and to me.

Sophie walked slowly into the house behind the girls, who were eager to introduce her to their grandmother. She wasn't so eager to meet the woman who would be *teaching* her how to take care of Simon's children and his house. Why was she so afraid? She'd never been afraid of anything in her life, but being here set her nerves on edge for some reason.

They stepped into the kitchen and Sophie looked around; a funny feeling came over her as if she'd been there before—standing on a chair—washing dishes at that sink. She walked over to it and looked out the window at the barn; wasn't there a red barn there before?

Sophie's heart raced, and she found it difficult to breathe. She coughed, hoping to catch her breath and Ellie rushed to her side.

"Are you sick?" she looked at her with worry in her small eyes.

Sophie managed to shake her head. "Maybe I need a drink of water."

Ellie pointed to the cabinet. "We have glasses in that one."

Sophie reached for the cabinet thinking she already knew the glasses were there—but how? She'd never been in this house before as far as she knew. Holding the glass under the faucet, she let it fill with water and then sipped slowly from it, trying to calm herself. Hadn't her father said the Yoders had bought this house twenty years ago? That would be about the same time as she and her father had moved from *their* farm.

She looked out at the barn again. Did she have a house just like this, or had her father sent her here because this was the house they used to live in? That could be the explanation but why wouldn't he just tell her? All he'd said was that after the summer, they were going to talk and he would answer all her questions about her mother. Was he hoping she would figure them all out if this *was* their old house? It couldn't have been; it had to be a coincidence. She looked out the window again; that barn was clearly white with a green roof and black shutters that matched the house. There was an old guest house beside the barn that she didn't recognize; it looked as if it had been around as long as the main house. Perhaps it was close to the house she grew up in, but it couldn't possibly be the same one.

He must think that farm living would jar some memories; he was right about that, but how much could being here help me?

An older woman struggled into the room with the use of a walker with wheels on the front. She had a kind face and attempted a smile despite the fact one side of her face was drooping. She'd seen her grandfather after his stroke, and he'd smiled the same way. Sophie smiled back, trying not to feel awkward around the woman.

"You must be the girl's *mammi,*" she said, trying to start on a good note—unlike her first impression with Simon.

The woman nodded. "Why don't you girls go out and pick some things out of the garden so I can have a nice talk with Sophie."

Ellie and Katie minded the woman immediately and exited the house despite Sophie wishing they could stay to help ease the tension she felt.

Mrs. Yoder motioned for her to take a seat at the table in the kitchen.

She sat but wondered if she should help the woman, who seemed to be struggling to sit. She stood up and reached out an arm to give her assistance, but the woman stopped her. "The doctor said I have to learn to do it for myself; *danki*—thank you just the same. The more I do for myself, the easier it will get. Three days ago I couldn't walk even a few steps. But today I can walk from one room to the other without too much trouble—thanks to this walker."

"I'm happy to see you're getting around so much better."

She finally landed in the chair with a thump, but she was sitting squarely. "It gets easier every day, and I'm grateful to *Gott* for letting me live."

Sophie smiled, thinking about how strange it must feel to be grateful for such a thing that she took for granted every day.

"I'm grateful for your help too," she said. "It was a *Gott*-send that your *vadder* came here last week and offered us your help."

I hadn't thought about it like that.

What had she been so worried about? This woman was kind—unlike her son, but she had to wonder if maybe he wasn't reserved like her own father. He'd never remarried, saying there would never be another woman like her mother and he couldn't imagine falling in love again. He'd claimed he'd had one great love in his life and that was more than some people have.

She wondered if she would ever find that same thing; being widowed worried her though. Widows surrounded her. Her father— and now Simon Yoder and his mother. She knew the pain in her father's eyes even after all these years. Sophie couldn't imagine loving someone so much that you spent the rest of your life missing them.

Was it that way for Simon?

"Did your *vadder* tell you that I would teach you to cook while you're here?"

Sophie nodded, sipping from the water she'd brought with her to the table.

"Did your *mudder* teach you when you were younger?"

Sophie shrugged. "If she did, I don't remember it. I was only five when she died; I don't remember her at all, and I can't get my father to tell me about her."

Sophie bit her bottom lip; she hadn't meant for that to spill out.

"Your *vadder* is still in love with your *mudder*," Mrs. Yoder said. "He's hurting like my Simon; he has shaved off his beard now, so I'm sure he will be ready to end his mourning period and start looking for a new *mudder* for the girls."

Sophie gulped her water, her face heating up. Was that the reason she was here? To become their new mother? The little one had mentioned she looked like her mother.

Oh no! Did my father bring me here to replace their mother and marry Simon?

He was handsome but not enough to make her want to marry him and become the mother to those girls he'd had with another woman; she wanted children of her own— didn't she?

"He's had plenty of offers from the women in the community, but he's rejected them all."

"Why?" Sophie didn't want to pry, but it seemed logical to ask. She hoped it wasn't because he was waiting for *her*.

"*Ach,* he's a stubborn *mann,* my Simon, but he'll come around, don't you worry. When it's time, he'll be ready to marry again."

Worry? Why should I worry about what Simon does or doesn't do with the rest of his life? I'm not going to marry him! But what will I do if he asks me?

"Your *vadder* told me you don't know how to do much since you were raised with a housekeeper and someone to cook for you; is this true?"

Sophie nodded, feeling shame heat her cheeks, but she was grateful the woman had changed the subject. She was here to help and nothing more. She was too young to be tied down to a couple of children who weren't hers and to a man who was as cold as Simon. She had her whole life ahead of her, and after the summer, she would have her trust fund to spend.

"The girls were so excited when they heard you would be coming to stay with them; they couldn't wait to meet you."

That seemed like a strange thing to hear, but she supposed it was so that some of the burden of the chores would not be on their little shoulders anymore, or was there more to it than that? Had they been told she would be their new mother?

"Why were they so happy to see me?" Sophie hadn't meant to ask that, but she couldn't stop it once the words left her tongue.

The old woman attempted another crooked smile. "They wanted to *wilkum* you to the *familye.*"

The family?

"I can't stay here! I have to go."

Sophie bolted up out of the chair, and it teetered against the wall behind her. Her heart felt as if it was going to explode from her ribcage and her throat was constricting. The room began to spin, and she tried to walk but collapsed back into the chair. Trying to stand again, her wobbly legs betrayed her, and she collapsed to the floor in a heap of darkness.

CHAPTER FIVE

Selma Yoder rose from the table as fast as she could and went to the back door to ring the dinner bell, hoping it would alert Simon. The poor girl had fainted, and she couldn't do anything for her without her son's help.

Reaching for the string, she moved the large bell back and forth until the clanging was loud enough to bring her son from the barn. "Hurry, the girl fainted on the kitchen floor!"

Forgetting all about his own worries, Simon rushed to Sophie's side, his heart racing. *Lord, let her be alright!*

He bent down and felt relief wash over him when he heard her breathing.

"What happened?" he asked his mother.

"I was telling her the girls wanted to *wilkum* her to the *familye,* and she bounced out of her chair and said she couldn't stay here and had to leave. The next thing I know, she's falling on the floor. I think she felt a little overwhelmed, the poor thing."

Simon wasted no time scooping her up into his arms; she groaned lightly, and he prayed she hadn't broken any bones when she fell. He took her back to his room to lie her down on his bed. "Get some meadow tea for her," he stammered to Ellie.

When he let her down on the bed, his cheek brushed hers when he pulled his arm out from under her. Kneeling beside the bed, he pushed back her blonde hair from her ashen cheeks. Her light frame had felt natural in his arms, and she smelled like roses. It made him nervous about being so close to her, but he feared for her right now. It felt strange seeing her in his bed; he never imagined he'd have another woman in his bed. Though he knew she would be staying in the room for the duration of her stay, he hadn't considered how it would affect him until just now.

Within minutes, Ellie was at his side with a cup of steaming meadow tea. How was he going to get her to drink it if she didn't wake up? He tried jostling her shoulder, and she groaned again. Her lashes fluttered, but she didn't try to speak.

He tucked his head under the back of her head, the warmth of her skin sending a charge through him. Lifting the teacup to her lips, he tried to get her to sip from it. She swallowed a bit of it, and her lashes fluttered again.

"What happened?" she said, barely above a whisper. "I feel woozy."

"You fainted and fell on the kitchen floor," Simon said. "Can you sit up?"

She lifted her head a little but then let it back down. "I can't; the room is spinning."

"You lie there and rest for a little while," he said, pulling her hand into his and squeezing it lightly. "I'll come back and check on you in a little while."

She held onto his hand and wouldn't let go. "I'm scared."

He sat on the edge of the bed and held her hand; how could he leave her when she needed him? "I'm right here if you need me."

She let out a sigh and relaxed, her grip on his hand loosening, but he couldn't leave her—not yet. He tried to tell himself that he was only concerned for her well-being, but he knew there was more to it, and for the time-being, he would allow himself to think about his attraction to her.

Sophie was aware of Simon's closeness though she couldn't stop from feeling dizzy unless she kept her eyes closed, but for reasons she didn't understand, she felt safe with him. Unlike Kyle, who seemed to have more than two hands when he'd tried to have his way with her. She'd felt comfortable in his arms, and she'd breathed him in just before he'd laid her down on the bed. He had a musky scent that most men would pay top dollar for, but she suspected it was his natural body scent. To her, it was a masculine scent, and it caused her to feel things she'd never felt before around a man. It tickled her that he was so gentle with her; it increased her attraction to him.

She allowed herself to relax a little and she felt his hand slip from hers. He rose from the bed, and she wished he wouldn't go, but she was certain he had better things to do than babysit her until the room stopped spinning.

She rolled over and opened her eyes; she watched him pick through his drawers and grab his things and pack them in a bag that was sitting on the top of the dresser. Then he went to the closet and took his clothes from there and stuffed them in the bag. He disappeared for a minute into the bathroom, and when he came back, he had a toothbrush and a razor. He stuffed those in the bag and walked toward the door, and then it dawned on her; he was giving up his room for her.

What a gentleman he is.

At the door, he turned back to look at her, and she closed her eyes, hoping he hadn't seen her watching him. What a gentle and giving man he was underneath that rough exterior. When he left, she pushed her face into the pillow that still held onto his manly scent and breathed in. A silly grin curved up her lips as she wondered what she was so afraid of.

Aside from fainting, she had nothing to fear—even if that was the scariest thing she'd ever experienced. His mother had said she was grateful to be alive after her stroke; now it was Sophie's turn to be grateful.

Thank you, Lord, for not leaving me when I needed you; I know I've turned my back on you for the past few years, but I'm going to change that.

Sophie sat upright, panic filling her for a minute until she realized where she was. Had she fallen asleep? The last thing she remembered was Simon moving his things out of his room and letting her stay. It felt strange that he should make such a sacrifice for her; she wouldn't do that for anyone, would she?

She threw her legs over the side of the bed and tried to stand. Her legs were a little wobbly, but she figured she could make it the few feet to the bathroom without falling. The dizziness had left her, thankfully, but she felt groggy. She closed the door behind her and splashed cool water on her face. Looking in the small mirror she assumed Simon used for shaving; she couldn't help but wonder what he thought of her. Did he think the same way as his young daughter and see his deceased wife when he looked at her? Would he want her for that reason alone? She didn't want him to; if he were going to ask her to marry him, she would want him to ask because of who she was, not because she looked like his wife.

What am I thinking? I don't want him to ask me to marry him! Do I?

She dried off her face and went to leave the bathroom when she spotted one of his shirts hanging on the back of the door on a hook. She pushed her face in the material and breathed in, a smile forming on her lips as she closed her eyes and breathed in again.

A knock at the door startled her, and she put the shirt down and swung the door open, relieved to find little Katie standing there looking up at her with her big, blue eyes that were the same color as her own. Sophie supposed their mother must look like her since they both had blonde hair and blue eyes—the same as she did.

That's a strange coincidence!

"I'm glad you're up," Katie said, her blue eyes sparkling. "*Mammi* told me to see if you wanted something to eat."

She shook her head, but her stomach growled, betraying her. She clamped a hand over her belly and smiled. "I guess it would be a good thing if I tried to eat something."

She wondered what time it was and how long she'd been in there, but she supposed it didn't matter. She seemed to have gained a little footing with Simon, so perhaps he wouldn't be upset with her for not helping.

After all, it was what she was there for, wasn't it?

When she exited the room, she could smell food, but it wasn't strong enough to indicate someone was cooking. When their cook made a meal, she could smell it strongly all over the house. Following Katie out to the kitchen, she was surprised to see Simon and his mother at the table and Ellie was at the counter serving the meal. She went over to the counter and offered to help, feeling awkward about not being there to help prepare it.

"I'm sorry I wasn't up to help you make this," she said mostly to Ellie.

She shrugged and smiled. "I didn't have to make it; Miss Anna brought it over for *Dat.*"

Sophie didn't know what to say, but she wondered who Miss Anna was.

Ellie leaned in and whispered. "She wants to marry *mei dat.*"

Simon cleared his throat and Ellie straightened up and finished piling the casserole onto the plate from the chair she was standing on.

"Why don't you let me do this, and you can pass them out," Sophie suggested, mostly because she wasn't ready to face Simon.

Ellie smiled and jumped down from the chair and held her hand out for the plate. Once Sophie had filled it with the noodle and chicken dish, she handed it to Ellie, who piled on a biscuit and took it over to her father. By the time she returned, Sophie had the next plate filled. Whatever the dish was, it smelled good, so even though she felt a twinge of unexpected jealousy about Miss Anna bringing Simon a meal, she was grateful she didn't have to cook it.

When she finished, she filled a plate for herself and sat down in the only empty chair which was next to Simon. She had to assume it once belonged to his wife, and she felt funny sitting there, but his mother had motioned toward it for her to use. Perhaps Simon wouldn't be offended—she could only hope.

She lifted her biscuit to take a bite but Simon bowed his head, and his family followed suit. She plopped the biscuit back onto her plate and bowed her head out of respect. He began the prayer, and she felt her cheeks heating up when he thanked God that she wasn't seriously injured when she fell.

Her father had not been a praying man, and so the bowing of her head was something new to her. She knew about God from a friend of hers she'd gone to school with, and she'd become a saved Christian at age sixteen. She'd tried to get her father to pray, but he claimed to have lost his faith when her mother died. It saddened her to the point she had let her faith fall by the wayside. Perhaps it was time for her to go back to the promise she'd made to God when she got saved. She'd promised that if she ever found out about her mother that she would devote herself to the faith and her new Christianity, and for a solid week, she'd tried to pry information out of her father. But at the end of the week, she hadn't worn down anyone but herself. From then on, she adopted his philosophy and gave up. Perhaps she'd gotten it all wrong; maybe she was supposed to believe *first* and then she would find out what she wanted to know.

Before Simon's prayer ended, she recommitted to her faith and made a new promise to God that she would have faith in him even if she never found out anything about her mother. She was too old to let that consume her anymore. She drew in a deep breath and let it out, thinking how liberating it felt just to *let go.*

She'd heard the saying *Let go and let God,* and she intended to do just that from now on.

CHAPTER SIX

Sophie woke up early to the sound of little fists knocking at the bedroom door to wake her. She looked up at the window, and she could barely see a trace of light through the curtains. Did they always get up this early? She hadn't protested when everyone went to bed early last night; she was wiped out after her fainting ordeal and then helping with all the dishes and cleanup after dinner. She hadn't ever remembered washing a single dish in her life up until the faint memory she had of standing on a chair the way Ellie did and washing dishes as she looked out at the red barn. She couldn't have been more than five years old in her memory, and she'd surprised herself at how quickly she'd picked it back up.

She looked over at the windup clock on the bedside table in Simon's room; it was only six-fifteen. She rolled over and pulled the pillow over her head to drown out the girls. It was only the second of June, and she had until August thirty-first before her father would be back to pick her up. Would she survive all the hard work until he did?

Hard work builds character; her father had said to her.

No, she thought; it makes you achy all over!

"Come in!" she hollered over their pounding.

The door swung open and the two girls, who had already gotten dressed, jumped onto the bed.

"Wake up, Cousin Sophie," they shouted in unison.

She bolted upright. "Cousin?" she squealed.

"*Jah, Dat* said you were going to be our cousin now," Ellie said.

Oh, okay, I get it. Sophie thought. *I should be happy with the word, cousin; at least they aren't calling me Mom!*

"Why do I have to get up so early?"

They bounced on their knees on the bed. "We have chores to do. We have to teach you how to milk Hoppy."

Her heart slammed against her ribs with a thud. "Is that your *cow?*"

"*Nee,*" Ellie said with a giggle. "Daisy is our cow, and *Dat* milks her because she's too big for us. Hoppy is our goat; we have to make some new goat cheese, so we need to get the milk from her."

Sophie bit her bottom lip trying not to laugh. "You named your goat *Hoppy?*"

"*Jah* because she hops around on the bales of hay in the barn and she climbs on everything!"

Sophie nodded. "Sounds like you picked a good name for her then."

Then her nose got a whiff of fresh coffee. She smiled. "Did you make coffee?"

Ellie shook her head. "*Dat* did; do you want some?"

Sophie nodded. "I can get it; let me get dressed, and I'll be out in a few minutes."

Sophie rose from the bed when the girls left the room, feeling a little unhappy that she had to get out of her comfortable pajamas and into the scratchy homemade dress, but her need for coffee put that to rest for now. Normally, she would lounge around in her pajama capris with the matching top and bathrobe while she had her morning coffee and often had her breakfast before getting dressed. She didn't feel comfortable doing that in Simon's house; he would probably reprimand her for it, and she wasn't up for that. The girls had already gotten dressed, so she assumed she would need to get dressed too.

Her stomach rumbled, and she was hoping she wouldn't have to make any breakfast, but she assumed they ate cereal like most other kids and had probably eaten before they woke her up.

She washed and brushed her teeth and then slipped into the dress once more, noticing it smelled a little musty. She hoped it would air out, but she'd have to wash it in the sink by hand and hang it over the edge of the shower overnight so it would be fresh when she put it on tomorrow. Mrs. Yoder had given her some material yesterday and offered to help her sew a dress this afternoon. How hard could this pattern be? She could probably have a new one sewn in about an hour. That would solve the dirty dress problem. Having a spare would help.

In the kitchen, she found the girls standing on chairs at the counter and mixing ingredients in a bowl large enough to swallow them. At the table, Mrs. Yoder sat peeling potatoes clumsily and cutting them into little wedges. She was missing helping again, and that was why she was there.

"What can I help with?" Sophie asked, feeling guilty they were working so hard and she hadn't done a thing yet.

Mrs. Yoder pointed to the stove. "Get a cup of *kaffi* first, and then we'll get you started on something."

She nodded to the woman. "Thank you! I feel a little groggy still this morning, but I'm ready to dive in and help."

Was that her voice she just heard saying she was eager to help? Had the bump on her head knocked her silly? She made up her mind right then that she would do what God wanted her to do today. If that meant working her fingers to the bone, she would do it. Wait a minute; what happened to her? Was it the eight hours of solid sleep she'd gotten, or perhaps she had a spring in her step from dreaming about Simon all night? Either way, she was determined to learn whatever lesson she had to in order to get through her summer.

At least this won't be as bad as summer camp!

She giggled inwardly as she poured a cup of coffee into a mug that Ellie handed to her. "Do you have any coffee creamer?"

"In the refrigerator," Mrs. Yoder told her. "Simon makes his own; I hope you like it."

She opened the refrigerator and then looked at the older woman. "How does the refrigerator work when you don't have electricity in the house?"

The girls had shown her how to use the gas lamps in each room.

"We have it running on propane," she answered.

"Wow! That's amazing!"

Mrs. Yoder chuckled, and she realized she was probably making a big deal out of nothing. She decided if she had any further questions, she would probably keep them to herself.

Sophie poured some of the cream into her coffee and took a sip. "That is tasty! He should bottle this and sell it to Starbucks!"

She hadn't meant to say it, but she seemed to be opening her mouth a lot since she arrived.

"I told him the same thing, but he's too busy with his buggy business," his mother said. "He got behind last year, so he has a lot of catching up to do."

Sophie had to assume he'd taken some time off after his wife's funeral, but she kept that to herself, not wanting to pry by asking such a question.

After a few more sips of her coffee, she asked what she could do.

"First of all," Mrs. Yoder said. "We work quickly because Simon is going to need his morning meal when he comes in from the barn with the morning milking. If we go too fast for you, step back and watch until you feel you can jump in and help. You can start by laying out strips of bacon on this cookie sheet; we'll put it in the oven so it'll cook at the same time as the potatoes. I'll have you put them in the pan and Ellie can stand at the stove and keep them turned, so they'll brown."

Sophie's heart did a flip-flop. Was it safe for the little girl to be at the stove at such a young age? She looked at Ellie, who seemed to be at ease in the kitchen and she had to figure that the girl had probably been helping in the kitchen for a few years already. Katie wasn't as much help, but she was certainly more help than Sophie herself was.

"After we get the potatoes and bacon cooking, you can start cracking a dozen eggs to scramble," she said. "Ellie, are you finished mixing up the batter for the streusel?"

She nodded, as she started scooping it in a square baking dish. Sophie went over and held up the large bowl for her so she could push it in the pan with the spatula. Then she sprinkled cinnamon on it and swirled it with a butter knife.

"Put some pecans on top for me while I rinse the bowl," Ellie said, taking the bowl to the sink.

Sophie dipped her hand into the Mason jar Ellie had open and grabbed a handful of pecan pieces and sprinkled them generously on top of the batter.

"Is it ready to put in the oven?"

Ellie nodded and opened the oven door for Sophie. "Put it on the top rack. The bacon has to go on the bottom."

She'd forgotten about the bacon when she'd seen that Ellie had needed help with the bowl, so she went back to putting the strips on the pan quickly and then popped it into the oven. In the meantime, Ellie already had the potatoes in the pan on the back of the stove, and they were starting to sizzle. Everything smelled so good it was making her stomach growl.

The girls continued to keep themselves busy with cleaning up the mess they'd already made. Ellie was standing at the sink washing bowls and utensils while Katie collected potato peels from the table where her grandmother had strewn them all over the table while she'd peeled them. She felt sorry for the girls; they worked so hard and they were so little. Wouldn't they rather go outside and play?

Sophie opened the fridge and got a bowl of fresh eggs; she could only assume the girls had gathered this morning while she was still sleeping. Guilt tore at her; she needed to step up and do all this work so they could just be kids. Maybe that was why her father had told her she didn't know anything about real work. These girls certainly knew what it meant to work hard. She cracked the eggs, and Mrs. Yoder told her to get a whisk and stir them, and then she set the iron skillet on the flame on low the way she had been instructed and let it get warm.

Opening the door to the oven, she checked on the bacon and the streusel, but she didn't want to close the door because it smelled so good. The combination of cinnamon and sizzling bacon made her mouth water.

Did they eat like this every morning? She was used to a bowl of fruit or sometimes cereal or a hard-boiled egg or two. She never had this much, and it worried her if she ate like this for the entire summer, she was going to go home with some extra weight on her.

"Do you always eat a large breakfast?" she asked.

Mrs. Yoder chuckled. "Don't worry; you'll work it off when you go outside and work in the garden!"

She hadn't thought about that; perhaps she would taste everything and see how it went. She certainly didn't want to make a pig of herself—especially not in front of Simon. But the kitchen smelled so good; she wasn't sure if she trusted herself to have restraint.

Sophie put the eggs in the pan and began to stir them immediately the way Mrs. Yoder instructed her. The girls disappeared with the egg bowl, and she watched them from the kitchen window while they went out to the chicken coop to gather more eggs. The potatoes where nicely browned and she'd turned down the heat to the *warm* setting.

"I think the bacon and streusel are ready to come out of the oven," she said.

Sophie gave the nearly-done eggs another stir and turned down the heat under them so they wouldn't scorch. So far, she'd been able to follow the instructions Mrs. Yoder gave her, and she couldn't help but think it wouldn't be long before she could do this herself.

Getting the potholders, she opened the oven and peered in at the bacon; it was done— a little crispier than she cared for, but it was done. She put it up on the middle of the stove between the burners and then took out the streusel and put it on the towel Mrs. Yoder had told her to fold and put down to protect the Formica counter top.

Simon walked in through the kitchen door carrying a pail of milk; he stood there staring at her for a minute as if he was frozen in his tracks. He seemingly caught himself and then set the pail on the counter without even looking at her, and it struck her as funny. Was he avoiding her after the way he'd treated her with such gentleness last night when she'd fallen? She'd hoped it wouldn't be awkward between them, but maybe it would for a few days; she would have to be patient until he warmed up to her and got used to having her around.

She let it go and silently gave it to God as she smiled inwardly, feeling too tickled to

let it bother her; she'd helped to make
breakfast, and it smelled wonderful.

CHAPTER SEVEN

Simon sat down to the meal and bowed his head for the prayer. He included Sophie again and second-guessed himself when he felt her eyes on him. He kept his eyes closed and finished his prayer, eager to eat the meal that he knew she'd helped to cook. He paused at the end, saying a silent prayer that the meal would be good because he was practically starving.

He poked his fork into his piece of streusel since it was his favorite; it was Becca's signature breakfast staple that he was happy to see his Ellie had learned from her mother before she passed. Ellie was going to make some man very happy when she grew up by feeding him that streusel for breakfast, and she would carry on her mother's tradition.

He put the bite of coffee cake in his mouth and closed his eyes against the cinnamon goodness that tickled him right down to his toes. If he was ever feeling down or stressed, Ellie knew her mother's streusel recipe was the thing to pull him out of his mood.

Ellie had filled his plate while he was eating his sweet treat and he picked up the bacon and held it out straight. "You overcooked the bacon a little bit this morning," he said to her.

"I'm sorry, *Dat,*" she said. "We left it to go out to the hen house to get the eggs."

He turned to Sophie and scowled without meaning to.

"I'm sorry," Sophie mumbled, fidgeting with her napkin. "I let the bacon get that crispy, I like it extra crispy; I should have asked how everyone else liked it."

He lowered his head, feeling like a miserable nag for complaining about her first meal. He would try his best to choose his words wisely if he could help it.

He bit into the bacon, and the taste surprised him. "Not bad; in fact, I think I like it."

She lowered her head and pushed the food around her plate, and that disturbed him; had he said the wrong thing? He thought he was complimenting her, but she didn't seem to take it that way. He groaned inwardly, wishing things were not so tense between them; he hoped that things would change as the summer progressed. It was only her second day, and from what her father had explained, he'd have to say she already fit in nicely. It pleased him that the girls had taken an immediate liking to her.

Then he took a bite of his eggs and the crunching set his teeth on edge. "I see Katie made the scrambled eggs again this morning," he said, forcing a smile.

"I made them," Sophie spoke up.

Katie giggled. "You made them with the shells, just like me, Cousin!"

Sophie smiled at the tot, but Simon could see he'd insulted her; he wished he could take it back, but what could he say? The damage had already been done. He put his head down and finished his food, eggshells and all; all he wanted to do was get out of the kitchen before he insulted the poor woman any further.

He picked up his plate and took it to the sink and left the kitchen without another word to anyone. The chatter had stopped and so had the eating; it was best if he escaped before the water-works started. The last place he wanted to be was in a kitchen full of emotional females.

He pushed his feet into his boots that he'd left at the back door and shouldered out into the hot sun that felt cool compared to the heat in the kitchen right now.

Sophie had never felt so humiliated in her entire life. Simon's insults had cut right through to her very core; was he even aware of how much he'd embarrassed her? The least he could have done was to apologize for his comments about the eggshells being in the eggs. But to compare her to his five-year-old's cooking skills was enough to make her call Kyle from her track phone and get him to pick her up. Here she thought the meal was going to be so good, and she was so proud of herself, but his insults had cut right through her. His comment about the bacon being too crisp had made her want to cry. She'd fibbed to cover up the embarrassment that she'd forgotten it and had left it in the oven too long. He'd patronized her by trying to say it was good, but she'd seen the look of surprise on his face; he was only trying to humor her. She was trying her best; couldn't he see that? She'd had to bite her bottom lip to keep the tears from spilling out. Was she ever going to get things right enough for him, or would she spend the entire summer messing up and making the wedge between them greater than it already was?

On top of it all, it was embarrassing that the girls were calling her their cousin; she was no more their cousin than she was their mother. How could she correct them without hurting their feelings? She supposed she'd have to live with the embarrassment rather than putting a wedge between her and them. At least they liked her, and it seemed his mother did too, but Simon ran hot and cold, and that confused her.

Mrs. Yoder touched her arm, and it pulled her from her reverie. "There is no reason for you to sulk about the meal; we're *familye,* and we don't hold anything against anyone here—especially if they are trying as hard as you have. I'm as proud of you as I would be if you were *mei* own *dochder."*

Family? Does she think of me as one of the family? What have I gotten myself into? I don't have any family—only my dad, and that's enough for me.

Sophie shook off the thought and began to clear the table; at least she discovered she wasn't too bad with washing dishes. Perhaps she'd stick to the dishes and leave the cooking to those who were more qualified than she was.

After the dishes were all washed and put away and the kitchen was clean, the girls dragged her outside.

"Do you want to weed the garden first or learn to milk Hoppy?"

Sophie looked at where the sun was, thinking it would be better to weed before the sun was overhead and at its hottest for the day. Besides, she would put off milking the goat for as long as she possibly could. As for making goat cheese; she'd rather go to the dentist, but she would never say that to them, or it would likely hurt their feelings. They were so excited to share it with her; how could she get rid of her resistance to it?

Lord, give me the strength to get through the day and help me to be open to trying new things without grumbling.

Sophie watched the girls remove their shoes and thick, long socks and walk in the garden carrying their galvanized pails and begin pulling weeds.

"Take your shoes off, so you won't get dirt in them," Ellie suggested.

Sophie hesitated; if she took off her shoes, her feet would get dirty. She remembered how dirty their feet had looked yesterday and figured this was how they'd gotten that way. She was thankful she didn't have to share a bathroom with them. She'd seen how muddy the bottom of the tub was after they'd had their bath before bedtime.

"No thank you," she remarked. "I think I'll leave them on."

"You'll get too warm if you leave them on," Katie said.

She was willing to take her chances. She watched them for a few minutes, admiring how hard they worked, but she felt sorry for them too. They dove right into the chore and knew exactly what they needed to do, while she felt a little lost. Except for the obvious plants with tomatoes or other vegetables already growing, she couldn't be certain she wouldn't accidentally pull out a plant thinking it was a weed. It was probably best if she stayed close to Ellie, who seemed to be making a clean path between plants.

"How do you know so much about the plants?"

"We planted all of it," Ellie spoke up. "*Mamm* taught us how, but we do it ourselves now that she's gone to Heaven."

Sophie wished she hadn't asked the question since it seemed to bring sadness to the girl's face that wasn't there a minute ago. She wished she had fond memories of her mother teaching her things, but as hard as she tried, she couldn't remember anything specific. She had a lot in common with the girls, but they were lucky enough to remember things their mother had taught them.

They could cook and clean and do the washing and weed the garden and pick the veggies from the garden; they gathered eggs and fed the chickens and told her how they plucked the feathers for eating them after their father butchered it. They could do all these things that Sophie couldn't do—all because they had a mother to show them. Had her mother taught her anything before she died, or had they not even been close?

She shook the worries from her mind and decided today was the day she was going to start learning—starting with taking her shoes off.

Stepping into the warm soil, she smiled, enjoying the feel of it on her feet.

"You were right; this is much better!"

Katie squealed, and Sophie turned her head as the child pointed to a tomato hornworm and began to cry.

"She's afraid of the tomato worms," Ellie said with an eyeroll.

Sophie went over to her and hugged her. "It won't hurt you; he's only a caterpillar."

"How do you know?" Katie sniffled.

"Because my mamma told me so!"

Sophie's blood ran cold as she realized she remembered being in the garden with her mother and her saying the same thing to her as a child.

She burst out a half-laugh, half-cry and tears filled her eyes. "I remember! My mamma told me they were harmless."

Sophie went to pick it up, but Katie squealed again.

"Don't let it sting you!" she cried.

"That might look like a stinger," Sophie said, putting her finger on the stinger-like end of the worm and showing the girls how flexible and harmless it was. "But see, I can move it from side-to-side, and it isn't even sharp. They have that there to scare off birds and other creatures who want to eat it."

"Ew!" the girls said at the same time.

"My mamma said that people fry these up and eat them!"

"Ew!" they said again.

Sophie let the bright green, fat worm crawl on her hand while the girls watched; she was too busy enjoying her memory to notice Ellie had picked it up and was playing with it.

Was this why her father sent her here? To remember?

"He's striped," Ellie said. "Will he turn into a butterfly?"

Sophie shook her head. "No, this one will turn into a moth, but they are quite beautiful and very big."

She thought about her memory some more, thinking that perhaps she was changing too—almost like a butterfly.

Simon stood in the doorway of the barn, leaning against the frame as he watched the girls in the garden with Sophie. He'd run toward the door when he'd heard Katie crying out, but he'd stayed back when he saw how well Sophie handled it. From where he stood, it had even looked as if she'd started to cry; was she that empathetic toward his daughters that she would take on their feelings? If so, perhaps things were going to work out after all with her, and he had nothing to worry about.

It did his heart good to stand there and listen to them giggling over a caterpillar in the garden as if they were already beginning to form a family tie.

CHAPTER EIGHT

Milking the goat turned out to be more challenging than Sophie thought; they should have named him kicker instead of Hoppy because he liked to kick. Once Ellie filled her feed bucket, she didn't kick as much, but it was not an easy task. One thing stood out; it required more than one person to milk the stubborn animal. The girls had put her in charge of holding her back legs, and the darn thing kicked her in the arm and left a bruise. They assured her the cheese was worth getting kicked, but Sophie didn't believe it for a minute.

She carried the large pail inside the kitchen for them because it was too heavy for the girls. They started to grab the handle together—probably how they were used to doing it, but Sophie took over for them. That's what she was there for; to lighten their burden.

Ellie got out another bucket and some cheese cloth and asked Sophie if she would pour it over into the other bucket to strain it. Once they did that, they put a big stew pot on the stove and turned the flame on medium. Sophie poured the milk into the pan, and they let it cook while they took turns stirring it to keep it from scorching on the bottom. It was late afternoon, close to dinner time, and their grandmother was still napping, so she hoped they were doing what they were supposed to be doing. Sophie had seen that the girls always had something to do, and she had hoped there would be time to start sewing her dress today, but they had spent too much time in the garden and had had to clean the house and milk the goat. She hadn't understood why every throw rug had to be rolled up and taken outside to be beaten on the clothesline until they began the actual task and the dirt flew in her face.

The two of them had put her to shame with the amount of work they could do while she kept having to take breaks. Every muscle in her body ached, and she was hungry constantly. Their grandmother had told her after a fast lunch of chicken salad sandwiches and strawberry shortcake that it was the fresh air that made her so hungry, but she believed it was all the hard work that she wasn't used to doing.

Ellie checked the thermometer they had placed in the pan. "Look, it's ready."

She turned off the burner and asked Sophie to take it off the stove and put it on the wooden trivet they had put on the counter.

"Now we have to put in the starter," she said.

"What is that?"

"It's like yeast that you put in bread dough," Mrs. Yoder said from the doorway. "We get it from Fork's General Store in town."

Fork's General Store? Why does that sound so familiar?

"Do they have little plastic bags with candies in them at Fork's?" she asked. "And shelves of fresh homemade noodles in clear bags—and nuts and other snacks—all homemade?"

Mrs. Yoder nodded and smiled. "*Jah,* they have quite a variety."

Sophie mindlessly watched the girls whisking the milk and put a lid on it. "I wonder how I knew that."

"Maybe your *mudder* took you there when you were little like me," Katie offered.

Sophie scrunched up her face. "I don't see how she could have."

"Your *vadder* said you grew up here," Mrs. Yoder said. "So you must have been there before."

Sophie felt her blood boiling; had he told the Yoder's about her childhood and her mother and planned to let *them* tell her about it?

How humiliating that they know things about me that even I don't know!

Sophie forced a smile and changed the subject. "What do you do with the milk now?"

"Nothing!" Ellie said. "We let it sit on the counter overnight; we will strain the curds in the morning when we get up."

Curds? Sophie thought she was going to gag.

Sophie had excused herself from the kitchen just before the tears filled her eyes; how could her father keep so much from her? Would she ever be able to forgive him? Mrs. Yoder had told her she grew up here; what did that mean? In the town? In the area? On the farm next door? What?

Angry tears poured from her eyes as she tried to make sense of it; was she so prideful that she couldn't ask Mrs. Yoder for more information about her childhood? If the woman didn't know any more than that, it would only disappoint her further, and if she did know more, then that would embarrass her. Either way, she was going to be hurt by her father's silence. She looked at the clock at the bedside table; she'd been in here more than ten minutes, and there was a meal to prepare. If she were gone too long, they would start to wonder, and she couldn't have them throwing her out on her ear before she found out what she needed to know about her mother. Being here was key to that knowledge; she was sure of that now.

Sophie splashed cold water on her face, forbidding herself to cry any longer; if the Yoder's didn't like her because she was so moody all the time, she would never be able to find out about her past, and she needed to know about her mother almost as much as she needed her next breath.

Simon had poked his head in the kitchen in time to watch his daughters making the starter for the goat cheese when things suddenly took a turn for the worse with Sophie. He'd seen the look on her face after she'd discovered a memory about her mother, and then she'd disappeared with barely a word. He'd gone back to knock on the door of his room to see if she needed anything and he heard her crying softly. He wished he could help her, but he'd promised her father that he wouldn't tell her too much too soon. He'd wanted to give her a chance to remember things on her own so she wouldn't feel he'd betrayed her by talking to Simon about it. That day that he'd come to visit, Simon had thought the man had gotten lost, but when his story of the past had begun to unfold, he knew that Hugh needed his help more than he needed Hugh's. A friendship had formed that day between them, and because of that, he'd agreed to take Hugh's daughter into his home with the hope that she would find the answers that she was looking for. It almost broke his heart that she was so confused and awkward on the farm when she should be a natural. Hugh had admitted the guilt of taking her away from the farm after his wife's funeral; he'd not been able to stay without the constant reminder of his loss. Simon understood that loss, but he couldn't just sell his farm the way Hugh had and move to the city. Hugh was an *Englisher* and had more schooling than he had. The only thing Simon knew was how to make buggies, and there wasn't much use for his trade in the *English* world.

Simon balanced the buggy wheel and then began to tighten down the spindles, making sure to put even pressure on all the spokes so it wouldn't wobble once it was ready for road use. He thought about Sophie's dilemma and wondered if she'd find her place here the way he was beginning to hope she would. She wasn't like the ladies in the community, who were practically throwing themselves at him ever since they discovered his mourning period had ended. Sophie had an innocent sort of spunk to her, and she seemed to put her foot in her mouth more often than she wanted, but he liked her raw openness. That, and her smile.

In the kitchen, Sophie was met with all smiles from the girls and Mrs. Yoder; she had to admit, it made her feel better. They were beginning to grow on her, and she prayed they would feel the same way about her.

"You're just in time to do the biscuits for me," Mrs. Yoder said. "I need to get up and stretch my legs."

Sophie felt lost. "What do I do?"

"Have you ever used a rolling pin before?"

She had with her Play-Doh set when she was young, but she kept that to herself. Instead, she shook her head and smiled.

Before rising from her chair at the kitchen table, the woman demonstrated how to roll out the dough. "Once you get it to about half an inch thick, use this round cutter and swish it in the pile of flour and then push straight down and swirl it a little to loosen the biscuit from the dough."

"I think I can handle that without a problem," she said, feeling suddenly confident.

Sophie stood over the table and began to roll out the dough while the girls chattered at the counter while they made a pitcher of fresh lemonade.

Their laughter lulled her into a memory of rolling out dough when she was little while she and her mother laughed at her biscuits that she cut too thick. Sophie stepped back from the table, feeling dizzy and she dropped the rolling pin on the floor. When it landed with a loud bang, it brought Mrs. Yoder back into the room.

Sophie looked up at the woman, her mouth falling open and her breath shaky.

"I'm sorry; It got away from me!" she stuttered, bending to pick it up from the flour-covered floor. "Don't worry; I'll clean this up."

When she stood with the rolling pin in hand, Mrs. Yoder had left the room.

Lord, please help me to stop being so clumsy; they must think I'm a crazy mess! Okay, maybe I am a little, but I don't know if I'm having flashbacks from my childhood or what, and I'm scared. Help me to adjust here with this family and pull my weight without messing everything up. And help me to forgive my dad for whatever he's keeping from me about my mother.

"Cousin Sophie!" Ellie said loudly, pulling her from her prayer. "Are you alright?"

"Um, yes—I was praying."

"Don't worry," she said. "*Mammi* isn't mad at you; she left the room to show you that she trusts you."

Sophie stopped shaking and drew in a deep breath, letting it out in a rush. That made all the difference in the world to her—more than she could say to the child. If she was trusted, then maybe she wasn't such a clumsy mess after all.

She washed off the rolling pin and then wiped the floor with wet paper towels and went back to work making the biscuits, remembering just how her mother told her to do it. It was refreshing to remember such a thing, but there were so many gaps in the memory it bothered her.

After cutting the biscuits and placing them evenly on the cookie sheet, Sophie popped them into the oven and went to answer a knock at the side door. Ellie and Katie followed her, fighting over who could get to the door first. Sophie took a large leaping step and got there ahead of them.

"That isn't fair," Katie complained. "You have longer legs."

Sophie smiled at them and then opened the door. The young woman standing there pursed her lips when they made eye-contact, and Sophie guessed she was Miss Anna from the basket of food in her arms, and that she was not happy to see Sophie there. She was a pretty, young brunette with striking green eyes and her appearance filled Sophie with immediate envy. So this was the woman who was her competition for Simon's heart?

"I'd heard Simon had a nanny," Anna said, her lips still pinched tightly.

"I'm not the nanny," Sophie said, annoyance showing in her tone.

"She's our cousin," Ellie spoke up.

Good girl! Sophie thought with a satisfying smile.

Miss Anna smiled and nodded. "I should have known you were *familye;* you look just like their *mudder.*"

"*Jah,* she's our *mudder's* cousin," Ellie continued.

"Yes," Sophie agreed, playing along. "*Not* Simon's!"

Anna sucked in her breath and furrowed her brow. "It hardly seems *proper* for you to be staying in the *haus* if you and Simon aren't *related.*"

"*Dat's* staying in the *dawdi haus,*" Katie offered.

Blabbermouth! Sophie fumed inwardly.

Anna let a satisfying smile spread across her lips, and it annoyed Sophie, but she wasn't about to let this young man-chaser off the hook that easy.

"Ellie and Katie why don't you take the food from her, so she doesn't have to stand there holding it," Sophie suggested.

"Thank you for the food," Sophie said. "But we won't need any more help; I'm here now, and I'm cooking for Simon and the girls." Sophie blocked the doorway, preventing the woman's attempt at stepping inside. "Have a nice evening."

Sophie closed the door before the woman could protest, and when she turned around, Mrs. Yoder was standing in the doorway and had witnessed the entire altercation.

Her breath hitched, and her cheeks flushed; her heart racing.

She opened her mouth to apologize, but the woman's face turned up into a smile.

"I've wanted to tell her for the past month to stop coming around!" Mrs. Yoder said with a light laugh. "*Mei* Simon isn't interested in her; she's too young and just wants to get away from her strict *vadder*. It's scandalous the way she's embarrassing herself by throwing herself at Simon the way she is."

Sophie giggled and then sniffed the air. "Oh no! My biscuits!"

She opened the door to the oven, and smoke rolled out the door. "Oh no; I ruined them!"

"We don't need them; Miss Anna brought some," Ellie said, unpacking the basket of food the woman had brought.

Sophie blew out a discouraging breath as she grabbed the tray of burnt biscuits from the oven and placed it on top of the stove. She waved the black smoke away, feeling humiliated that she couldn't cook.

"Now we don't have to cook," Ellie said.

Sophie felt guilty for the way she'd treated Anna, even if she was a little jealous. "I'll thank her next time I see her."

Ellie rolled her eyes. "That'll be tomorrow; she's been coming every day except Saturday and Sunday."

"For how long?"

"More than a month," Mrs. Yoder said.

Sophie smirked. "She must be exhausted doing all that cooking."

"She makes extra when she cooks for her *vadder*," Mrs. Yoder added. "I'm sure she's been hoping for an invitation to join the *familye* for the meals she brings, but Simon has no intention of inviting her."

That put Sophie's mind at ease, but she wasn't exactly sure why.

CHAPTER NINE

Simon bowed his head for the prayer over the meal; he wouldn't embarrass Sophie again by including her. Instead, he made it as general as possible. When he finished, he took a bite of the fried chicken and complimented Sophie on a good meal before he remembered he hadn't butchered a chicken today.

She seemingly ignored him, and he hoped she hadn't heard him.

"*Dat,* we didn't make supper tonight," Ellie said. "Miss Anna brought it over."

He cleared his throat and didn't dare look at Sophie, but he could feel her eyes boring a hole right through him.

"What did you girls do today?" he asked, hoping to avert the subject away from his mistake.

"We started some goat cheese," Ellie said. "We can have it with supper tomorrow since Miss Anna probably won't be back."

Simon raised his eyes from his plate and looked around at the table full of females who suddenly seemed to be a little too interested in the food on their plates at the moment. "Why is that?'

"I'm afraid it's my fault," Sophie blurted out.

"I don't think Anna likes the idea of Sophie being here," Mrs. Yoder interrupted her.

"Well, I don't know about everyone else at this table, but I think we can do without her pestering us from now on," Simon said. "I know she thinks she's doing us a favor, and the food has been a blessing, but she's doing it for all the wrong reasons, and I don't want any part of that. If she stops bringing us food, I think we can be thankful for that."

He looked up in time to see an exchange of glances between his mother and Sophie, and though he wondered what it might be about, he wasn't sure if he wanted to open that can of worms before he'd had his supper. Maybe it was best if he left the female matters to the ladies of the house—especially since they seemed to be getting along just fine without him getting in the middle of it.

Some things, he thought, are better left alone.

Sophie almost ratted herself out to Simon, who would have sent her packing for sure if she had. During his prayer, she'd asked for forgiveness for the way she'd spoken to

Anna and promised God that if she saw the girl again, she'd apologize to her.

Thankful that his mother saved her from making a fool of herself in front of Simon, she still wondered why she kept it from him. As a mother, did she think it was for his own good that he didn't know all the details, or would she tell him later in private to avoid embarrassing her to her face? Sophie prayed she would not tell Simon what she'd done. She'd asked for forgiveness, and she prayed it was behind her now.

After they cleared the dishes from the table and all the leftovers were put away, Mrs. Yoder asked to speak to her privately.

Oh no! Here it is; I'm getting my walking papers!

She held her breath as she followed Mrs. Yoder into the sitting room while the girls did the dishes. Simon had gone out to the barn to bed down the animals for the night, and so it was just the two of them.

Did she really care if she was going to get canned? Not completely; she'd never wanted to come here in the first place. But now that she had, she wanted to stay so she could have more memories of her mother since they seemed to stem from her visit to this farm.

Were they connected somehow? She put the thoughts away as she sat in the opposite rocker in front of the fireplace; even though it wasn't lit, it was a pretty place to sit. She imagined it would look lovely in the winter with a roaring fire going and pine branches to decorate at Christmas, but none of that mattered because she wouldn't be here to see it.

"I suppose you're wondering why I didn't tell Simon what you said to Anna," she said.

Sophie stopped squirming in the chair and looked over at her. "I am a little curious, but I was going to confess the whole thing to him."

"The women in the community have been bringing him food ever since his Becca's funeral, and it's been a constant reminder of his loss," she said. "He's been unable to move on because they are a constant reminder, and they push him to make the decision to remarry when he isn't ready. Only he will know when he's ready, and it won't come for him unless he's at peace. These young ladies steal his peace, and that is why I didn't correct you earlier."

Sophie nodded.

"The women here have learned that he has ended his mourning period and Anna has pushed out all the others by making it known she intends to pursue Simon; I heard it from her cousin, and I don't approve of her pushiness, so for setting her straight, I appreciate that."

Sophie didn't know what to say.

"I am wondering why you spoke to her in that way; are you interested in pursuing my Simon?"

Sophie felt the blood drain from her face as she twisted at her apron strings. She didn't know how to answer that question because in some ways she was very attracted to Simon, but in other ways, she felt reserved. She would never admit to his mother that the thought of marrying Simon had crossed her mind or that she had stuffed her nose in his shirt and felt things she wondered if they were love or just infatuation.

She shrugged knowing the woman was waiting for an answer she couldn't give.

"I think it's a smart match with the two of you—if you should think in that direction, but only time will tell if it is meant to be," the woman said.

"Mrs. Yoder, I hope you don't think that…" her voice trailed off. What could she say that wouldn't be a lie?

"Please, call me Selma," the old woman said.

"That's a pretty name."

Selma smiled. "*Danki.* So is the name Sophie—it's unusual. Not a name you would normally hear in the Amish community."

Sophie did a double-take, wondering what the woman meant by the comment, but she let it go. There were more important things to discuss; she could see it in the woman's eyes.

"When *mei familye* first moved here twenty years ago—Simon was only seven years old then, and his *brudders* were twelve and fifteen—Simon was a bit of a late surprise for *mei* husband and me," she began. "I remember thinking this was the *haus* for *mei familye,* but maybe it would have been better off if the *familye* who sold it to us would have stayed. I remember the barn was red when we bought it, and *mei* husband thought it was prideful to have a red barn, so he painted it. I miss that *mann* and his funny ways; Simon is a lot like him."

Sophie remembered looking out the kitchen window and thinking she'd seen a red barn there before. Had she ever been here before—maybe when she was younger? She couldn't pull the memory from her mind even if it was there—which it wasn't. The glimpse she'd gotten of the red barn could have been from anywhere.

"Do you remember much about your *mudder?*"

Sophie swallowed the lump that instantly swelled her throat at the mention of her mother. "My father has never talked about her much more than a sentence here and there, and I've exhausted him with questions he refuses to answer. I barely have any memory of her; shouldn't I have *some* vivid memories? I mean, I was five years old—almost six when she died, but I don't remember anything. It makes me feel bad for Ellie and Katie because they are about the same age I was when I lost my mother; do you think they'll remember their mother?"

Selma nodded and smiled sadly. "*Jah,* Simon is *gut* about talking to them about her— no matter how much pain it has caused him, he makes certain that they know as much as possible, so they don't forget her."

Tears dripped down Sophie's cheeks. "I wish—my father—would do that—for me," she sobbed.

Selma held out her arms and Sophie went to her and cried against her shoulder. "Why can't I remember more than a few little things, and why won't my father tell me about her?"

Selma smoothed her hair that had come loose from her bun. "Because he's hurting. He's afraid that if he talks about it, he'll have to admit she's really gone."

"But he's wasted his whole life being unhappy because he misses her so much," Sophie cried. "And he's made me miss out on knowing anything about her—except what I've remembered since I've been here."

She continued to sob for a few more minutes and then she asked to be excused; she was exhausted and didn't want to have to face Simon when he came in from the barn.

"You get some rest," Selma said quietly. "And don't worry so much; forcing the memories won't bring them. They will come when *Gott* feels you're ready."

Sophie accepted that explanation and went off to Simon's room to go to bed for the night.

Sophie picked wild berries and plunked them into a small pail until it was almost full. She'd eaten almost as many as she'd put in the bucket and her mother laughed at her.

"You won't have enough for the pie you're making for supper," she said, her blue eyes sparkling in the sun.

It was a beautiful summer day, and the sun was warm on her skin; Mamma's light blue dress fluttered in the warm breeze, and her skin glowed in the bright sunlight.

She handed her mother the lilacs in her tiny fist, and she smiled, the sun forming a halo behind her mother's light hair.

"Mamma, did you go to Heaven?"

Her mother nodded. "Promise me you won't forget me."

"I promise."

Sophie bolted upright in the bed, her breath heaving; she drew up her knees and hugged them, rocking in the bed as she sobbed. "Oh Mamma, I broke my promise! I don't know how to remember you; I don't know where my memories went."

She stopped crying suddenly, grasping onto a thought; in the dream, she'd picked the lilacs from the side of the Yoder's house—her house! She had to know if they were there; she had to know the truth.

Wiping her face and sniffing back the tears that threatened to keep flowing, she pulled on her robe and exited the room, noting the clock on the wall read midnight, and the house was silent. She tip-toed to the front of the house and turned the knob on the front door as slowly as she could so the creaking wouldn't disturb Selma or the girls.

Once she was safely outside, she went to the far end of the porch and leaned over the rail and breathed in the fragrant lilacs. She giggled sadly as she remembered her mother's face in the dream, realizing she must look just like her mother—unless her dream was only a dream and not a memory.

But that wouldn't explain how she knew the lilacs were there.

Her heart beat wildly; had she dreamed what she did because she'd seen the lilac bushes there already, or had she known they were there all along?

"What are you doing out here so late?"

Sophie's breath hitched as she turned around to face Simon, who was still dressed, except for his hat and shoes.

She drew in a breath to steady her racing heart and sniffed back happy-sad tears that threatened to give away her emotions.

"You wouldn't understand," she said, without thinking about it.

"I think I do," he said. "I couldn't sleep either; I was having bad dreams, and I came out here to think."

"I had a *good* dream," she said. "But I'm confused because it was bad too."

He motioned toward the swing for her to sit while he took a seat on the rocker beside it. Sophie sat and rocked her bare feet back and forth heel-to-toe, causing the chain to squeak just a little. She stopped to listen to the crickets, who seemed unusually louder than in the city. Fireflies lit up the humid night air as they fluttered around the yard.

"I wouldn't blame you if you wanted me to leave," she said.

"I promised your *vadder* I'd help you," he said gently.

Sophie raised her eyes until they met his. There was kindness in them.

"To remember," he answered. "It seems as if it's working."

"I knew that the lilacs where there on the side of the porch," she said, pointing behind her. "How did I know that?"

"You must have remembered them from when you lived here."

Sophie jumped up from the swing, her limbs shaking. "When do you think I lived here?"

"When you were a little girl; your *vadder* said you moved away after your fifth birthday—after…"

"After my mother died," she said, her voice breaking. "Why did he tell you and not me?" she sobbed.

"You mean you didn't know?" he asked.

Sophie shook her head. "What else don't I know about? Am I really your daughter's cousins?"

He nodded his head slowly and Sophie collapsed onto the swing and buried her face in her hands, unable to hide her sobs.

CHAPTER TEN

Sophie had a million questions, and Simon didn't seem to have any of the answers, and he could see the frustration in her eyes.

"We met the *familye* that sold the farm to us, and I will never forget the look on the little girl's face as her *vadder* drove away from the *haus;* it was blank—as though the life had gone from her. I found out later that she'd been in a buggy accident with her *mudder,* and her *mudder* was killed."

Sophie looked at him funny—soberly.

"That little girl was you, Sophie!"

Sophie's breath caught in her throat, and a cry escaped her lips. "No!" she sobbed. "My father would have told me that; I'm sure he would have."

"He told us that he never told you how she died," Simon admitted. "I was only seven years old when *mei vadder* bought your farm, but I hadn't forgotten you in all those years. I felt sorry for you. When your *vadder* came to visit us last week, I was more than happy to help you. Then when I saw you that first day you were here, I didn't know how to relate to you because it seemed as if you looked at me with that same blank stare."

"I wasn't happy to come here," she said, sniffling. "My father *made* me come; he fed me a story about learning good work ethic and how much you needed my help."

"That part is true; until *mei mudder* fully recovers, I do need the help."

"Back to what you just said; who told you I was in the accident with my mother?"

"It was in the newspapers," Simon answered.

Sophie sniffled and wiped at her swollen, red-rimmed eyes that broke his heart when he made eye-contact with her.

"Can I go into town to look up the archives at the library?" she asked. "Wait; where is *town* from here?"

Simon pointed behind her. "It's that way about twelve miles. I can take you on Saturday."

"Do they have a library there?"

Simon nodded. *"Jah,* I've borrowed books about bee-keeping and hydroponics."

"I didn't know the Amish were allowed to read—um—I mean—I'm sorry, I didn't mean that." He could see her face turn red by the light of the full moon.

"It's alright; I know what you meant; there are a lot of misconceptions about the Amish. You'll see when you start to learn more about the community."

"Wait a minute!" she said, holding up her hand. "Does this mean I'm part *Amish*?"

Simon nodded and tried to smile, hoping she wouldn't see being Amish as a bad thing. "You mean you didn't know?"

She shook her head. "I thought your girls were joking with me when they called me *cousin.* Am I really their cousin?"

"*Jah,* you and their *mudder* were cousins; that's my understanding from what your *vadder* said. So you and the girls would be second cousins I think—it may be further out because I'm not *gut* with figuring out how far out a cousin is—you might be once-removed."

"Did my father tell you if I have any other relatives around here?"

"*Nee,*" Simon said. "I'm sorry; he was pretty vague."

"Yeah, he's been that way with me my entire life! Did their mother have any relatives that might be related to me too? Any that might know more about my mother?"

"*Jah,* she has many, but I have no idea how they might be related to you."

"Can I meet them?" she asked eagerly.

Simon let out a sigh knowing she wasn't going to like his answer. "We don't see them much anymore since Becca passed away. We don't attend the church anymore or any of the gatherings that take place. I've cut myself off from the community because I wasn't going to join the church. *Mei familye* moved here when I was young, and we have no relatives here; we moved to get away from our church. When Becca married me, she was shunned by the community because she had already taken the baptism into the church and I refused the baptism."

"Why didn't you join?"

"*Mei vadder* chose to break away from the church and the old order, and I grew up in the community but not a part of the church. It gave *mei vadder* the freedom to live as he wished, and I prefer the same. *Jah,* I keep in contact with the Bishop, and we are *gut* friends, but he knows I have no desire to join."

"So the girls don't see any of their extended family?"

"They see Becca's *mudder* and *vadder* regularly, but because we don't visit very often or attended church, we don't see the others as often. Her parents broke away from the church too so they wouldn't have to shun Becca."

"Do you know if my mother had any close relatives here—like parents or siblings?"

Simon ran a hand through his thick hair; she was asking the question Hugh hadn't shared with him. He'd only told him about the girl's relation to her, and that wasn't enough to go by. He couldn't give her false hope, but he didn't want to upset her either.

"I can ask Becca's *mudder;* she might know; I don't have the answers you're looking for, but I think Lettie Beiler could help you. I can invite her over, and the two of you can talk. Beyond that, I don't know because Becca's extended *familye* shunned her when she married me. They shunned her for leaving the church."

"That must have been heart-breaking for her."

"It was their choice and beyond her control," he answered.

He could see by the look in her eyes that she was not happy with his answers; he was exhausted, and her questions were wearing him out.

"I'm sorry if it hasn't been easy for you to have me here in your home."

He forced a smile. "You caught me off guard the first time I saw you; I had no idea you would remind me so much of Becca."

"I'll bet now that you know me a little better I don't!" she said with a smirk.

He chuckled lightly. "You're right about that; she was quiet and reserved, and you have a bold personality—but it works for you."

"I hope that was a compliment!"

Simon nodded. "It was. I need to get some rest; I have chores to do in only a few hours, but I'll run by the Beiler's place after the morning milking; it's the next farm up, the opposite way of town."

"You mean they live next door?"

He chuckled. "Not next door; it's a couple of miles up the road."

She nodded and rose from the swing. "Your daughters are early risers, so I better get some sleep. Plus if I'm going to meet the Beilers, I better have all my questions ready for them."

She paused as if she wanted something more from him, but he wasn't sure what. He resisted the urge to pull her into his arms and comfort her, but he wasn't sure he trusted himself not to want more from her. But that didn't stop him from thinking it; had she paused for the same reason?

"Good night," she finally said, her voice straining.

He nodded and left the porch and went around back of the house to retire to the *dawdi haus* before he gave in to temptation.

Sophie made it through breakfast without a hitch, and she was pleased with her efforts; what she wasn't pleased with was the fact that Simon had gotten too busy to speak to the Beilers but had promised to go after breakfast. She was anxious to meet them, but she wanted so much to learn everything she needed to learn about her heritage, and she wanted to impress Simon, but he seemed preoccupied and wasn't paying much attention to her this morning.

"We're going to teach you to sew a dress today, Cousin," Ellie said.

She looked at the young girl and smiled; now that she knew the truth, that word meant so much more to her.

My cousin; I have a family after all, and I'm going to find the rest of them if I have to turn this community upside down!

Lord, please let the Beilers have the answers I need to find the rest of my mother's family.

"What color do you want to sew?" Ellie asked.

"I think blue would be nice and it would match my eyes," Sophie said. "What do you think?"

"So you can marry *mei dat?*" Ellie asked with a giggle.

Sophie felt her face heat up. "No!" she said. "Why would you say that?"

She glanced across the table at Simon, who'd lowered his gaze, his face reddening.

"Blue is for weddings."

Sophie cleared her throat. *Okay, I should have seen that coming!*

"You and Katie are wearing blue dresses," she pointed out.

"But we are too young to get married," Ellie said.

"She can make a blue dress without getting married," Selma corrected the girls. "If that's what color she wants; that's what we'll make."

Sophie flashed Selma a thankful smile for bailing her out of the tight spot the girls had put her in. It wasn't that she didn't like the shy look Simon flashed her for about half a second, or the idea of marrying him; truthfully, it was starting to grow on her.

They cleared the dishes, and Selma asked the girls to wash them by themselves so that she and Sophie could get to work on her dress. She was glad they were finally getting around to making a dress and hoped it wouldn't take too long because she was tiring of washing her single dress every night in the bathroom sink and hanging it up over the shower to dry overnight. Selma had given her a cake of laundry soap that was tearing up her hands because it was so strong; she'd told her it was homemade lye soap. She preferred the lavender soap in Simon's shower and had used that on her dress last night. She was looking forward to learning how to make the soap with them on Saturday, but Simon had promised to take her into town to visit the library if Lettie Beiler wasn't able to help her. Then, she could look at some of the newspaper archives about her mother's accident.

She'd thought a lot about what Simon had said about it, and it seemed strange to her that she wouldn't be able to remember such a thing. Surely, if she'd been in an accident that killed her mother, wouldn't she have *some* memory of it? It seemed logical that she would, but it was as foreign as her mother herself was to Sophie. She didn't have much feeling one way or the other except to feel sad that she'd missed out on knowing her. That, and the fact that her father had kept the information from her all her life.

Sophie entered the sitting room with Selma, who instructed her to pull open the cedar trunk under the window to get the fabric, needles, and thread.

"Get the measuring tape so I can take your measurements," Selma said.

Sophie brought it to her and asked where she could find a pencil and sheet of paper to write them down.

"I don't need to write it down; I've been doing this all my life, and I haven't made a mistake yet."

Sophie believed her, but she wondered if her mind was still the same since her stroke. Rather than insult the woman, she was determined to help the woman remember her measurements so that she didn't end up with a dress that didn't fit.

She stood still and turned when Selma told her to.

"That didn't take long at all," she said. "You're the same measurements as Becca was so we can use her old patterns from the bottom of the trunk; will you get them out?"

"What do they look like?"

Selma pointed as if that made a difference. "They're in the bottom; there's a false bottom in the trunk."

Sophie dug everything out and set it on the floor to get to the bottom of the trunk. She lifted the thin piece of wood from the small cutout and there they were.

"Which one do you want?" she asked, turning to Selma.

"Bring the pile here, and I'll pick the best one."

Sophie did as she was told; once Selma made her choice, she returned all the items to the trunk and went back to get her instructions. Selma showed her how to lay out the pattern pieces onto the fabric and had her pin the paper pattern to the fabric. Because of her limited mobility with her hands, Selma was unable to show her most of the tasks, so it took Sophie the better part of an hour to pin two pieces. Her fingers ached, but she didn't complain once; she was that eager to have a new dress.

"Why don't we take a little break and see what the girls are up to," Selma suggested.

Sophie was happy to get up from the floor; her neck and back were strained from hunching over the fabric. She had a long way to go, but she was making progress. She had no idea that making a dress was so tedious, but she was excited about it, nonetheless. Selma told her that cutting out the fabric and piecing it together would probably take several hours; she couldn't help thinking it might take her *days* at the pace she was going. She tried not to feel discouraged because she knew it was a process and it was not going to happen in an hour the way she thought only days ago. It amazed her how much she'd already learned; wouldn't her dad be surprised when he came to get her at the end of the summer?

Thinking about leaving filled her with panic; everything would change once she left. She wouldn't get to see the girls every day—or Simon either. She would certainly miss Selma too; she'd become close already and almost felt like a stand-in mom. Would they want her to leave when her time was up?

Then she realized she hadn't thought about her trust fund even once for the past twenty-four hours. Would she still want it when the summer was over? From what she could see, Simon would not be interested in sharing it with her. He was a humble man—not to be confused with a simple man. He was anything but simple; he was the most complicated man she'd ever known, but she liked the idea of spending the rest of her life discovering all there was to know about him. Was he even looking for a wife, or were the women in the community trying to push him into something he didn't want? She certainly would not pursue him; not that it mattered because he was seemingly ignoring her. She could only guess that it was because he felt awkward after their talk last night on the porch.

If she could get away with it, she'd go out there again tonight. He did say that he goes out there to think in the evenings. Perhaps she'll have to meet up with him again—just to see where things might go.

CHAPTER ELEVEN

After two hours of weeding the large garden with the girls, Sophie was ready for a nap, but they had to get lunch ready for Simon, who hadn't come back from the Beiler's farm yet and she was beginning to get nervous. He'd waved to the girls before he left, but he seemed satisfied his girls were keeping busy and under her care, so he left without a word. Was he always that quiet and reserved? Somehow, she doubted that; after hearing about his reluctance to join the Amish church, she could see some spunk in him, and she liked that. He was handsome and caring, and seemed to have a big heart; he would probably make a good husband. She had finally admitted to herself that she was interested, but would he accept her now that he'd learned she was Amish?

She let out a sigh. *Not unless I can learn to cook and clean and sew like an Amish woman. Those little girls put me to shame with all the things they know. How long will it take me to learn, Lord?*

Grateful that the midday meal seemed to consist of leftovers from the previous night, she knew they could get through the warming up and serving rather quickly. She was eager to get back to her dress-making after lunch. One thing was certain; the Yoder family was certainly on an awfully tight schedule for people who didn't leave their property. Her father often worked at home, but even he wasn't as diligent as the Yoders.

"Can we have a picnic today, *Mammi*?" Ellie asked.

She nodded and gave her a crooked smile. "That would be lovely."

"I'll set the picnic table," she said. "Katie, get a table cloth from the pantry."

The girls set to work and were so excited; it put excitement in her too. It was a beautiful summer day, and she couldn't remember the last time she'd had a picnic. Although she wasn't sure if she could call eating on the patio under an umbrella with her father a picnic, she supposed it was in a way. She'd sat on the fountain in the center of the college campus plenty of times with her roommate eating Subway sandwiches, so she supposed that was a sort of picnic too.

She giggled inwardly thinking about what her friends would think of her after they learned she was Amish, and the thought of it didn't worry her in the least. Admittedly, it was a bit of a shock at first, but for some reason, when she woke up this morning, it almost seemed like a relief to finally know something about her past—even if it was a little unusual. Perhaps she was finally growing up the way her father had said she would. He'd been right about things not being the same for her after being on the farm, but she didn't think it would happen this quickly. Knowing she used to live here was still a puzzle for her since she didn't really remember anything significant about it, but she prayed that would change in time and she'd get back the pieces of her life that seemed to be missing for so long. Now that she'd met Simon and his family, her life would never be the same again, but that was a good thing; wasn't it?

Sophie looked at her new family; even if things between her and Simon didn't amount to anything more than friendship, at least she had the girls—her new cousins.

"Wait for me!" she called to the girls as she grabbed the potato salad out of the fridge.

"Look at all these beans we picked from the garden!" Sophie showed off the large bowl to Selma.

"It's such a nice afternoon. Why don't we sit on the porch and snap them," she said with a smile.

"Snap them?" Sophie asked.

Selma looked at her with wide eyes. "You've never snapped beans?"

She shook her head. "I'm willing to learn."

"That's all that matters." Selma smiled again, and Sophie noticed the sagging in her face had improved, and she was pleased to see the change.

She'd been working hard, and she'd gone from clumsily peeling potatoes to being able to get through an entire spud before having to take a break. And they were clean; Sophie hadn't had to go over any of them after she finished. Even her walking had improved some; she was able to go up, and down the ramp that Simon had built over the kitchen steps without as many breaks. Being outdoors today had worn her out though, and the girls had worked out in the garden some more after lunch.

Now that she was up, perhaps after they snapped the beans, she would be able to work on her new dress a little bit. She was eager to have a new dress before she met the Beilers. Simon hadn't told her yet when they were coming to see her, or if they would, but she prayed she'd be ready if, and when they did.

The girls each grabbed a couple of extra plastic mixing bowls from the cupboard and raced out to the porch ahead of Sophie and Selma. Once they were all situated, Sophie divvied up the beans, and they showed her how to snap the ends off and separate the snapped pieces into one bowl and keep the snapped ones in the other bowl. It was easy enough, and Sophie was grateful for the chance to sit for a few minutes. Her back ached from the garden work and scrubbing the kitchen floor on her hands and knees with a scrub brush. She'd never worked so hard in all her life, but she had to admit, it almost seemed more like fun than it did work. Yes, her back told her it was work, but the girls had a way of making things fun, and she wasn't sure how they did it. It was almost like playing a game.

When Sophie had finished snapping her portion, she went inside to get some lemonade and cookies. "Should I take some to Simon in the barn?"

Selma nodded and smiled. "I think he would like that. It'll give you a chance to see how things went with the Beilers; I know you're eager to find out."

"Thank you!"

Sophie felt almost giddy for the chance to be alone with Simon, even if it would only be for a few minutes, but she also had to know if the Beilers could help her. She hurried to get Selma and the girls their refreshments and then poured a glass for Simon and tucked a few cookies into a napkin for him. She walked slowly toward the barn practicing what she would say once she'd given him the cookies, but anything she could say was sounding foolish in her head. If he was more talkative; she could rely on him for a bit of small talk, but he had been quiet since they'd talked on the porch. Talking had been easy last night because it was dark, but it was full daylight, and there wouldn't be anything to hide her pink cheeks if she should feel embarrassed.

The barn door was open, and she called out to him. "Hello! Simon?"

Just inside the door, there was a work bench, and she set the refreshments down there and walked further into the barn, passing a couple of stalls until something caught her eye. A carving on the post toward the bottom made her crouch down to look. She traced her finger over the word.

Charlie.

Whinnying from behind her brought her to her feet with a jolt, her heart racing. "Charlie Horse!" she cried out. Her limbs shook, and she felt dizzy. "Charlie Horse," she repeated. The horse whinnied again, and she closed her eyes and fell to her knees in the soft hay. She could hear the sirens and Charlie horse was hurt. "Mamma, Charlie Horse is dying!" she cried out. "Mamma? Oh no, Mamma please don't leave me!"

Sophie curled up in a ball on the floor and sobbed as she rocked back and forth unable to process the memory. "No, Mamma, no!"

She felt a strong pair of arms go around her and pull her close while she sobbed.

"It's alright," Simon said, smoothing her hair. "You're safe now."

"Charlie Horse is gone," she cried. "My Charlie Horse died in the accident too, didn't he?"

"He did," Simon said. "I'm sorry."

"Why was I the only one who lived through it?"

"It was my understanding that you had gotten thrown from the buggy on impact and you had a head injury," he said, still cradling her sobbing frame in his arms.

"Do you think that's why I can't remember much of anything?" She leaned up from his shoulder and looked into his blue eyes that filled her with a sense of safety.

"That's what your *vadder* told me; he was hoping that being here would help you to remember everything. He said the doctors tried for two years and you had to learn to walk and talk all over again. The doctors said you forgot everything leading up to the accident."

"Then how did I remember just now? I remember hearing sirens and seeing Charlie horse, and my mother on the pavement and they weren't moving, but just before that, I heard Charlie whinnying—more like squealing."

"I wish I could explain that to you, but maybe this is a breakthrough for you, and it means that you're on your way to remembering the *gut* stuff too."

She sniffled, and he reached up and wiped the tears from her cheeks. His lips parted, and he cupped his hands around her face and drew her toward him until his lips touched hers. Her head felt fuzzy, his lips pleasurable against hers as they swept from side-to-side deepening the kiss. Her limbs tingled, and a warm fiery desire for him coursed through her. She loved him; she wanted to be his for the rest of her life.

"Take your hands off my girlfriend!" a shout startled them.

Simon was on his feet before she realized that Kyle was standing in the doorway of the barn, hands on his hips and an angry look on his face. Simon extended a hand to Sophie and helped her up.

"I'm not your girlfriend, Kyle," she said while she brushed the straw off her dress. "What are you doing here?"

"I got worried because you didn't answer your phone and I come out here to check on you, and I catch you kissing this—this Amish dude!"

"His name is Simon, and you didn't need to check on me because I'm fine. I didn't answer because there isn't any electricity in the house, so I couldn't charge the phone."

Ellie and Katie came rushing into the barn and ran up to her and threw their arms around her.

"It looks to me like you're here playing house with this guy and his kids!"

Sophie raised an eyebrow at him. "I'm not playing; it's for real."

He lifted his phone and snapped a picture of her before she could raise her hands to cover the girl's faces.

He laughed a mean laugh. "This one is going on Facebook, so you can kiss all your friends goodbye."

"If they'd un-friend me over something like this, then I wouldn't consider them friends—just like you and I aren't friends anymore."

"I can't believe you teased me for more than a year and wouldn't give it up, and here I find you shacking up with this guy!"

"Stop it, Kyle," Sophie said. "Please go!"

"I think you need to leave," Simon spoke up.

"You know he only wants you for a mother for his kids," Kyle said. "I'm here to rescue you from that."

"I would consider it an honor if he'd let me be their mother," Sophie said. "And I don't need rescuing—especially not from you."

His mouth hung open, and his eyes widened. "Are you serious?"

"Yes, I'd like you to leave now."

He pointed to Simon and scoffed. "This dude has you brainwashed into taking care of his family."

"They're *my* family, and I'm staying here; this is where I belong."

"Sophie, you've lost your mind!" Kyle said closing the space between them. "I'm taking you with me if I have to take you by force!"

Simon stepped between Kyle and Sophie; he stood his ground against the short, spindly Kyle. Simon had chosen a short-sleeved shirt that morning, and it showed off his large muscles.

Kyle threw his hands up defensively. "I thought you people were peaceful," he grumbled. "I don't want to fight you, Dude!"

"I will defend *mei familye,*" Simon said with a gruff voice.

Kyle pointed to Sophie and shouted; "You're crazy!"

And then he walked out of the barn and down the driveway to the end where he'd left his car. He hopped in, slammed the door and squealed his tires as he peeled out of the driveway. He sped off, and Sophie stopped shaking.

"Are you alright?" he asked her and the girls.

They all three nodded and told him yes. Simon pulled them into a group hug and kissed Sophie on the forehead, pausing there as he sighed loudly.

"Girls; go in the *haus* with *Mammi,"* he said. "I need to talk to Sophie for a minute."

Once they were gone, Simon still hadn't said a word. Was he angry that Kyle had said he was her boyfriend? He looked tortured; as if he wanted to take back what just happened between them.

Her throat began to swell and tears formed behind her eyes; he was upset because of what Kyle said, and he was going to break up with her before they even had their first date.

She couldn't stand the silence any longer. "Kyle isn't my boyfriend," she blurted out. "I dated him a couple of times, but we've stayed friends because we don't have anything in common as you could clearly see."

"I believe you," he said soberly. "But I need some time to process what happened between us. I think I acted on impulse kissing you, and now I'm fighting feelings that I betrayed Becca's memory with you."

Sophie bit her bottom lip; she was not about to cry and make a bigger fool of herself than Kyle just did.

"I hope you understand that I need time to think," he said softly.

She nodded, her lips pursed. "I understand."

She walked away from him, unable to stay near him another minute without breaking down and crying. Her heart was breaking, and she couldn't do anything to stop it. She'd told him she understood, but it had not been the truth; she didn't understand how he could kiss her like a man in love and then turn around and practically take it back.

She almost wished Kyle would have stayed long enough for her to pack her things and go with him.

CHAPTER TWELVE

Simon hated to say what was on his mind, but the last thing he wanted to do was to hurt Sophie by leading her on. He'd let himself get caught up in the moment, and now he felt awful. He wouldn't blame her if she wanted to leave; he hadn't missed the tears welling up in her eyes when she walked away. He'd wanted to pull her back into his arms and kiss her like a man in love, but he couldn't—not yet. First, he had to sort out his feelings and decide if what happened between them was impulse or if he had real feelings for Sophie that didn't stem from loneliness or from feeling sorry for her in the moment.

He was attracted to her; that much he could admit, but was it enough to kiss her the way he just did?

He paced the floor of the barn grasping at any thought that would make sense of what just happened, but he couldn't get one that worked. He felt a twinge of jealousy over Kyle; had she kissed *him* before? The man had accused her of teasing him and refusing his advances. At least that's what he thought the guy meant by his crude remarks. Did that mean she'd been saving herself for marriage? He saw her as that type of woman—conservative and respectful of herself and others, but she was an *Englisher,* and there seemed to be a lot of promiscuity in the *English* world.

He guessed what it all boiled down to was only one question; did he want her to leave or did he want her to stay? He rolled his shoulders trying to loosen the stress in them. Of course, he wanted her to stay—if not for him—for the girls' sake. Running a hand through his hair, he let out a long sigh; what had he done? He'd kissed her like she was his wife and she wasn't.

His cheeks burned. *How could I let that happen? I know better.*

He continued to pace, his shoulders sagging. It was no use in trying to figure a way out of this mess; he'd hurt her, and he doubted she would give him another chance.

Sophie ran into the house not thinking about what she would find when she entered the kitchen so hastily. Her breath hitched when she saw the girls sitting at the table with Selma eating their snack, and they were all smiles.

"We got you some lemonade and cookies," Katie said with innocence so sweet, Sophie had to bite her bottom lip to keep from letting her tears let loose.

"Thank you—*danki,*" she said without much thought.

Where had that come from? Had she spoken like that as a child or had being there begun to wear off on her speech too?

Selma flashed her a look. "Do you want to talk?"

Sophie forced a smile, but her quivering lower lip betrayed her.

Selma looked at the girls. "You're done; go out to the garden and pick some fresh tomatoes for supper."

They picked up their plates and cups and took them to the sink; they were so obedient.

Sophie lowered her gaze. "I'm sorry that Kyle showed up here; I hope you're not mad at me, but I gave him the address before I came here thinking I would need someone to come get me in case things didn't work out."

"How did Simon react to him being here?"

Sophie covered her face with her hands. "I thought the two of them were going to fight! Kyle said some really inappropriate things and I think Simon felt he needed to defend me—or

164

maybe he was defending himself too; I don't really know. He's not my boyfriend; he's not my friend anymore and he won't be back."

"Did he come to get you?"

Sophie nodded without lifting her gaze. "I considered leaving with Kyle for a minute—but that was after…"

Her voice trailed off.

"Did something happen between you and Simon?"

"I think he wants me to leave!" she cried.

"I doubt that," Selma said. "Do you want to tell me what happened?"

"He said I reminded him too much of Becca and he feels he's betraying her memory."

Sophie felt her cheeks burning; she hadn't meant to say that, but she was so upset she wasn't thinking straight.

"How did he betray her memory?" Selma asked. "Did he ask you for a buggy ride?"

Sophie looked up at her, confusion clouding her mind. "Buggy ride?"

Selma smiled. *"Jah,* that is what Amish do when they are courting."

Her eyes widened. "Ohhhh! Um, no, he didn't ask me for a buggy ride, but I was crying because I had a memory of the accident and my horse, Charlie, and he *comforted* me."

Sophie could feel her heart trying to beat its way out of her ribcage; she didn't want to confide in the woman, who'd felt like a mother to her since she'd been here, but she had to talk to someone, or she was going to make a rash decision that would probably involve leaving the farm. She was bursting with emotion, and she needed some advice, even if it wasn't what she wanted to hear.

Selma put a warm hand on hers and patted it. "I wouldn't worry so much; Simon will come around when he's ready. I see the way he looks at you; there is a longing there in his eyes, but there is also fear. He's pushed away every young woman who has made herself available to him for marriage, but with you it's different. He might need some time to sort out his feelings."

"That's what he said to me—that he needed time."

"Well, then your job is to be patient and wait if that is what you want."

Sophie didn't have to think about it; she had fallen in love with him. She didn't know when or how it happened, but her feelings were strong.

"I suppose I have some thinking of my own to do," she said.

"Why don't we work on your dress," Selma suggested. "Keeping our idle hands busy will help."

Sophie rose from the table and excused herself to wash her face. If she could make a new dress it would make things easier for her, and Selma was right; she needed something to occupy her, so she didn't overthink the situation.

"Am I doing this right?" Sophie asked. "It seems to be bunching up in the corners."

"Unpin the end and lay the fabric flat on the floor and slip your hand underneath to hold it while you pin it. I'm afraid it's going to be a while before I can hold something as small as needles and pins or I'd demonstrate for you."

"I'm never going to get the hang of this," she grumbled under her breath.

She held it out in front of her and tried to smooth it out, shaking her head at the mess she'd made of it.

Ellie set down her quilt square and sat on the floor beside her. "Take out these pins and start over," she said with such patience it put shame in Sophie that she'd felt so rushed. "If you pin it too tightly, you will cut it to thin, and it won't fit over your arms."

She let out a heavy sigh. "Maybe I'm just not cut out for this."

Katie sat at the little table by the hearth playing checkers by herself, and Sophie felt so frustrated right now she'd almost rather go over there and play with her. She was growing impatient and wanted to finish the dress so she could wear it, but she hadn't even begun to cut the fabric out yet. If she could only get the sleeves pinned, she'd get there, but right now she was over it and ready to give up for the day. Not to mention she couldn't keep her mind on task; the only thing on her mind right now was that kiss between her and Simon. It warmed her insides to think about it.

"You'll get it," Selma assured her. "You should have seen my first dress; it would have fit a tall tree, but it didn't fit me."

Sophie laughed. "What did you do?"

"I took it apart and started all over again, and I kept trying until I figured it out. It took me three tries."

"I hope it doesn't take me that long or this dress I'm wearing is going to rot off my bones!"

Selma laughed. "I don't think it will take you that long; maybe a day or two."

"I have a couple of more work dresses in the trunk in the attic if you want one to spare," Selma offered.

She blew out a loud breath. "I better not; I promised my dad I'd make one. If I let you give me another one it would feel a little like I failed. Even if it takes me a week, I'm committed to making this one. If I give up now, I'll never learn."

A knock at the door interrupted her worries about the dress, but her heart thumped at the thought of a new worry that could be on the other side of the front door.

"It's them!" Sophie squealed. "I hope it's them!"

Sophie jumped up and went to the door, and the girls were on her heels.

"*Mammi, Pappi,*" they shouted, holding out their arms for hugs.

Sophie peered into the pair of blue eyes that seemed almost familiar to her.

"You must be Sophie," the woman said, her voice strained and her eyes misty. "I haven't seen you since you were a wee one like Katie."

Sophie felt numb as the woman pulled her into a hug; her mind reeling, trying to pull the questions she had to the front of her mind, but it all seemed to leave her all at once.

"I'm sure you're anxious to hear about your *mudder,*" she said sitting on the sofa. "I'm Lettie Beiler, and this is *mei* husband, Amos; your *mudder* and I were very close."

"What was her name?" Sophie managed, lowering herself slowly beside Lettie.

"Your *mudder's* name was Laney Bontrager."

Sophie felt strange now that she knew; she mulled it over in her mind for a minute, trying not to cry. "I didn't even know her name!"

"You lived in this house, and your *mudder* loved gardening and growing flowers. She grew her own herbs to make homemade soap. You look just like she did at your age. What would you be now? About twenty-five?"

Sophie nodded, feeling her throat constrict. "My father wouldn't tell me anything about her, and he sent me here to work for Simon without telling me I used to live there when I was a little girl. He didn't even tell me how she died; I had to discover it for myself."

"She died in a buggy accident twenty years ago."

"I figured that much out by remembering Charlie Horse."

"Did you get your memory back?"

Sophie hugged her back, trying to hold back the tears. "No, I only remember bits and pieces of the house and the accident."

Lettie continued to tell her stories about her mother over the next hour during her visit, but Sophie got the feeling the woman was holding something back. She and her mother had been neighbors, but she had the nagging feeling there was more that Lettie wasn't telling her.

Sophie helped the girls clear the table after supper. She was glad the meal was over because it had been so quiet you could hear everyone chewing their food. She'd pushed most of her meal around her plate and waited until Simon excused himself to bed down the animals for the night so she could toss the remains of her meal in the trash. She didn't like wasting food, but she had no appetite; Simon had refused a second helping, and that surprised her since he had such a big appetite.

Selma had tried to engage him in conversation a couple of times, but it fizzled out quickly with the short answers he gave her. If this was how things were going to end up between them, Sophie didn't think she was going to be able to take it for long before she made up her mind to leave. It was the last resort, but her stomach was so tight she needed the silent tension to end.

"You and Simon are going into town day after tomorrow, *Jah?*" Selma asked.

Sophie nodded as she filled the sink with hot sudsy water. "That's if he'll speak to me by then."

"Give him time; he'll come around, and when he does, I'm sure everything will be alright."

Sophie shrugged; she wished she could be as confident as his mother was, but she knew him best. Hopefully, she knew him well enough to be right about him; she needed Selma to be right because her heart was going to break if this lasted much longer.

"You might ask Simon to take you to the Bishop," she offered. "He might remember your *mudder,* and he might be able to tell you more than Lettie was able to."

Sophie's eyes brightened. "That's a good idea! I hope he'll have time to do both."

"He takes the weekends off to run errands and to spend Sunday with the girls."

Sophie stared out the window at the sinking sun; she wondered if he would include her in his family day on Sunday. If not, then perhaps it would give her some time off so she could finish her dress. She would have liked to have it ready for their trip into town, but she doubted she would finish it by then. There just weren't enough free hours in the day to work on it.

Ellie and Katie finished clearing the table and stood on either side of her at the counter. They looked up at her wistfully, eyes as big as saucers. "Can we go outside and catch lightening bugs? We promise we'll come back in and help you with the dishes as soon as we get some; we want to put them in a jar and use them for a nightlight."

Sophie smiled; how could she say no to those faces? "Of course you can, and don't worry about the dishes; I'll do them tonight. Have fun and stay close to the house."

She looked over at Selma for approval. "I'm sorry; should I have asked you?"

Selma shook her head. "*Nee,* you are in charge of them, and you're doing a *gut* job."

"Thank you; that means a lot to me."

Selma rose from her chair and excused herself to go and sit in the other room, leaving

Sophie to her thoughts and the dishes, neither of which she wanted to deal with now. She had a nagging thought that Lettie was not telling her everything she knew about her mother, and it made her want to talk to her again.

Sophie finished the first sink-full of dishes and decided to go out and check on the girls. She walked through the front room where Selma was snoring lightly in her chair. She slipped out the front door without making a sound, not wanting to wake the woman. In the yard, she spotted the girls immediately, and they were minding her and staying close to the house; that made her happy to know that they respected her enough to obey her. She lowered herself onto the swing and watched them play, wondering if things would change between them if she were lucky enough to win Simon's heart.

"I caught one!" she heard Ellie squeal.

A man's laughter caused her to sit up and take notice; it was Simon.

"Put him in the jar," he said to his daughter.

She sat there and listened to him playing with the girls and his laugh made her giggle; it made her happy to hear him enjoying his time with them. She imagined it was something she'd like to hear for the rest of her life. She was certainly in love with him, but she feared he would be unable to return her feelings.

Simon laughed again with the girls, and Sophie couldn't help thinking it was the most wonderful sound she'd ever heard. She admired how he was with the girls and knew what a loving man he was; if only he weren't so afraid of getting too close to her.

CHAPTER THIRTEEN

Sophie had managed to get through breakfast and lunch without a single word to her from Simon; was he ever going to talk to her again? Sure, he'd made small talk, but she didn't consider asking her to pass him the biscuits talking to her. Of course she didn't expect him to talk about their personal encounter in front of the children, but she was dying to know what he was thinking and feeling.

Did he even know?

Though he'd not been unkind to her in any way, he hadn't looked at her once during either meal. Then after he'd finished his first helping of food, he'd rushed out of the house as if his pants were on fire. His mother had talked to him and so had the girls, but she didn't dare utter a word for fear she'd break down and cry and ruin mealtime for everyone.

Lord, bless me with an extra measure of patience for Simon; I want an answer from him that he's not ready to give. Help me not to push him before he's ready, so he doesn't make the wrong choice.

She mindlessly washed the dishes and placed them in the strainer for the girls to dry and stack them on the counter. When she finished, she put them all away in the cabinet and wiped everything down, so it sparkled. At least she'd gotten the hang of cooking and cleaning—as long as the girls and Selma were at her side ready with instructions if she needed them.

"Will you run out to the garden and pick out a vegetable for dinner?" she asked the girls.

"What do you want?" Ellie asked. "Beans, broccoli or corn?"

Sophie laughed. "Even I know the corn isn't ready yet! You better get some cucumbers, tomatoes, lettuce, and celery. I think we should make a salad to go with dinner."

They grabbed a wicker basket by the back door and ran outside to do her bidding. She had to admit; a salad sounded refreshing; it amazed her how much she was enjoying the fresh varieties of fruits and vegetables from the garden. She could certainly get used to this life; growing her own food and raising children to be self-sufficient.

She watched from the kitchen window while Katie chased a butterfly around the yard and Ellie tried to get her attention away from it to pick the vegetables from the garden. Simon exited the barn and Sophie covered her cheeks with her hands and stared out at him, a pain stabbing at her heart.

She smiled, though tears filled her eyes. She blinked them away and sniffed, jutting out her chin and decided not to cry. She would trust God to make things right between them if it was meant to be, and she would not pressure Simon.

"How long are you going to stare out that window?" Selma asked.

Sophie's hand flew up to her chest, and her breath hitched as she turned around to face the woman. "You scared me half to death!"

Selma smirked. "Sorry, but why don't you go out there and talk to him?"

"No! I can't do that; I promised I'd give him some space."

"He's had plenty of time to decide what he wants," Selma said. "You don't have to press him for an answer, but he's never going to be able to decide unless he spends time with you talking like normal people. It's not *gut* this silence that's between you."

"But he won't talk to me," Sophie complained.

Selma chuckled. "I don't see you talking to him either; you're just as stubborn as he is. How do you expect to solve this if neither of you is willing to talk to the other?"

"I agree, but I don't know what to say; I'm not good with conversation when it comes to matters of the heart. I suppose that's why I never had a boyfriend."

"One of you has to be the first one to speak," she said. "Trust your heart, and trust in *Gott*."

Sophie sniffed back her tears and splashed cool water on her face. "I'm ready; I just pray the Lord will give me the right words to say."

"Have faith," Selma said. "It will work out; however it's supposed to."

Sophie dried her warm cheeks and headed out the door when a strong breeze whipped her dress, and it caught in the crease of the screen door, ripping the skirting across the back when she yanked on it. She squealed and gasped at it, trying to pull it loose and trying to cover her backside from exposure. "Oh no! I'm stuck!"

"Push the door open all the way," Selma said from the kitchen table, where she'd sat down. "It looks like it got caught in the corner."

Sophie pushed against the door to open it fully, holding the back of her dress against her slip. She went back into the kitchen in tears. "What am I going to do now? My new dress isn't finished."

"Come over here and turn around and I'll see what it would take to repair this one."

Sophie went to Selma and turned around; the woman clucked her tongue and sighed heavily. "I'm not sure we can fix this to make it look right; you managed to tear it in a sort of zig-zag, and I'm afraid it would bunch up in the back and be too short. We're going to have to replace the whole skirt, but it's an old dress and not worth all that much trouble."

Sophie's breath hitched. "I don't have anything else to wear!"

"I'll have to send you up to the trunk in the attic to get another one of Becca's old dresses."

Sophie gasped. "You mean this dress used to belong to her?"

Selma nodded matter-of-factly. "Well, *jah,* where do you think it came from? We didn't make it for you. I had the girls bring it down from the attic, and when your *vadder* looked at it, he said it would fit. And if it needed altering, he could get his housekeeper to help with that."

Sophie sucked in her breath. "I knew it was a used dress, but I didn't know I was going to come here reminding him so much of Becca because I was wearing her clothes!"

"It's not as bad as you're making it out to be," Selma said. "Simon knew we had gotten the dress for you and he understood. He was going to donate them to the ladies in the community, but he hasn't gotten around to it. Here in the Amish community, we understand the value of helping others, and that includes donating clothes and food to those in need."

Sophie twisted her apron strings and bit her bottom lip, fixing her gaze on Selma. "Will I need to wash it before I can wear it?"

"Nee, they're in a big plastic bag; they got washed before I put them away and they haven't been disturbed except to get you that one."

"Where is the trunk?"

"It's in the attic; the door is at the end of the hall upstairs."

Sophie followed Selma's instructions and went upstairs to the attic. She immediately found the trunk right near the door and opened the lid. On top was a large plastic bag. Unfolding it, she removed the dresses from inside, and her eye caught the light blue dress on the bottom of the stack. All the others were the same dark dresses like the one they gave her. She'd wanted a blue dress so badly and could not bring herself to wear another brown dress. She wanted to look pretty for Simon when she went to talk to him.

Holding it out in front of her, she swished the soft fabric, the skirting shimmering in the sunlight from the window behind her. The delicate white collar looked to be the same material as the girls' prayer *kapps,* and it complimented the simple but beautiful dress. Lifting the torn dress over her head, she let it fall to the floor in a crumpled pile and then slipped into the blue dress. She smoothed down the skirt and smiled; it was a perfect fit—almost as if it had been made for her.

"*Danki,* Cousin Becca for the beautiful dress!" she said as she twirled.

Her eye caught a glass door at the front of the attic, and she walked toward it, thinking she remembered the door. She stood in front of it and looked down at the yard; she'd been forbidden to open it and stand on the widow's walk. Her parents were afraid she'd fall. She smiled at the memory, happy to have another piece of her puzzle. She opened the door, and it creaked loudly as if it hadn't been opened in years. Below, the girls were in the yard with Simon and they looked up when she walked out onto the balcony. She lifted a hand to wave and Simon bolted toward the porch. Thinking he might not want her out there, she walked back inside and closed the door.

Closing the door to the attic, she made her way down the hall when Simon came running up the stairs. He stopped when he saw her; he was out of breath, and his expression was pained.

"It was *you* standing out there!" he said with a raised voice.

Her heart sped up at the sight of his twisted expression.

"Of course it was me; who did you think was standing out there?"

"Take that dress off!" he demanded.

Sophie looked down at the dress and felt her blood run cold. "What's the matter?"

"I said take that dress off; now!" he said, his voice breaking.

"I don't have anything else to wear," she said. "My dress ripped, and your mother said I could get another one out of the attic."

"If you have nothing else to wear, I'll give you a grain sack to put on, but I want you to take that dress off immediately!"

"A grain sack?" she squealed. "Why are you treating me this way? What did I do wrong?"

"Take the dress off!" he said and then turned on his heels and walked hastily down the stairs and out of the house.

Sophie ran down the stairs, her breath coming out in heaving sobs.

Before she reached the kitchen, Simon met her in the hallway and tossed a grain sack at her feet. "Put that on!"

"I won't!" she cried, pushing past him and out of the house.

She ran down the driveway sobbing, the girls chasing after her calling out to her.

Sophie kept running despite hearing Katie's sobs as she called out her name.

Simon caught up with the girls in the middle of the long driveway and scooped Katie up into his arms; she was sobbing hysterically and still calling out for Sophie.

"She didn't wait for me!" Her breath hitched when she tried to speak.

"I'm sorry, Katie, it's my fault she left," he soothed her.

Ellie looked up at him, tears filling her eyes. "Is she coming back?"

His heart felt like it fell to the ground in a bunch of broken pieces. He could see in his oldest daughter's face that she loved Sophie. It was too late to admit it, but he was pretty sure he did too. They'd be lucky if she came back after the way he treated her. He hadn't meant to get so upset, but when he'd seen her up on the widow's walk, he thought it was Becca at first. She used to stand up there and wave to him and blow kisses at him from up there. Seeing Sophie up there in that dress stabbed at his heart and he hadn't handled the situation right.

He wished he could have walked away from the situation and taken the time to think before he reacted, but it was too late for that. Now that she knew which direction town was, she would likely go there and call her father to pick her up—or maybe Kyle. His stomach wrenched and his throat felt tight; he loved her so much it hurt.

He lifted his eyes heavenward. *Lord, forgive me for the way I treated Sophie just now. You know why I reacted badly, but she doesn't; she probably thinks I hate her and that I'm a crazed maniac! Please tell me if I should go after her; please put forgiveness in her heart for me and give me the courage to tell her I love her.*

CHAPTER FOURTEEN

Simon walked back up to the house and took the girls into the kitchen, his mother giving him a look.

"I already know I didn't handle that the right way and now that I'm calmed down, I'm going after her; please keep the girls inside."

Katie bounced on her heels and dried her eyes. "Bring her back home where she belongs," she said. "Tell her I love her."

"Me too!" Ellie chimed in.

"Me too! Selma added.

"Me too!" Simon admitted.

His mother opened her mouth to speak, but he put a hand up. "I know, but I hope it's not too late."

He ran out to the barn and hitched the buggy so he could go after her and bring her home; his only problem was convincing her he loved her.

Sophie stopped running when she realized Simon had reached the girls before they'd left the driveway. She hated leaving them this way, but she couldn't stay on the same property as that man a minute longer. How dare he give her a grain sack to wear like she was some kind of poor, country girl who didn't have two pennies to rub together. So what if it was about to be true! She'd failed to stay even a full week at her job, and for that, her father would cut her off. So much for her trust fund taking care of her for the rest of her days; now she'd be stuck being a secretary or something menial at her father's company until he was done punishing her for failing at the only thing that he'd asked her to do. And that was if he felt generous; she'd probably get stuck in the mail room.

But what of him? He'd kept her whole life from her; surely that was worth enough guilt to make him rethink her trust fund. Who was she kidding? She didn't want the money; she'd wanted Simon—until he started having a meltdown over a stupid dress. She looked down at the pretty fabric and liked the way it felt on her; much better than that itchy dress they'd given her. Why hadn't they given her *this* dress?

When she reached the end of the driveway that seemed to stretch an entire mile, she paused; the town was twelve miles away, but Lettie Beiler was less than three. Would the woman take her into town if she should show up on her doorstep? They'd had such a wonderful visit, and she'd promised to visit with her again soon, but Sophie couldn't wait. She needed more answers, and she felt as if the woman was holding back something from her. She didn't want to leave the community when she was so close to finding out about her mother, but she didn't want to be around Simon right now either.

She turned toward Lettie Beiler's place, her footsteps pounding heavily against the pavement; her clenched were hands bouncing up and down with her angry steps. With heaving breaths, she stomped along the road, determined to walk the twelve miles into town if she had to, just to call her father and demand he that come and get her. Her shoulders sagged when she thought about leaving; she loved the girls—and Simon too. Would he let her see them now that he'd been so harsh with her? Her lower lip quivered; she was going to miss the girls, and Selma; the woman had been so kind to her—almost like the mother she never had. As for Simon; she loved him, and she didn't know how to keep her heart from breaking.

She heard buggy wheels from behind her, and the clip-clop of horses hooves and her pace eased up and relaxed; so Simon had come after her! She didn't turn around; she wanted to wait until he was right alongside her to see what he had to say for himself. She would give him the chance to apologize and then she would forgive him. Hopefully, that would end the feud, and he would allow her to keep the dress that she loved so much. Giddiness rose from her gut; she loved him so much, and it pleased her that he was going to give her the chance to stay.

When the buggy stopped far behind her, she gave up hope Simon had come after her. Disappointment and pride kept her from turning around; seeing it wasn't him would only rub salt in her wounded heart.

When she reached the next farm up the road, she had to assume it was the Beiler's farm since it was the only one as far as her eyes could see along the flat stretches of road. But there was something else; the windmill she'd stopped to look at on the way here was at the far end of the property; she knew that windmill for some reason, but what could it be? She'd been to this farm, but when? Was it another memory she'd blocked out?

She began to shake; if she'd been here before, then she was right about Lettie not telling her everything. What was she hiding from her—and why?

The front door opened, and Lettie walked out onto the porch and called to her.

"You look like you've seen a ghost!" Lettie said.

Sophie looked up, her cheeks feeling flushed. "I think I have; I've been here before, haven't I?"

Lettie nodded. "With your *mudder.*"

"Why? When?" she could hear the desperation in her own voice, but she needed answers.

"When you were little—before your accident. I'm your *mudder's schweschder*—her sister."

Sophie felt her blood run cold and her wobbly legs began to betray her; she stumbled toward the porch and Lettie met her midway and pulled her into her arms. They both sobbed and held each other for some time until Lettie walked them toward the porch. They sat on a wicker settee together, and Lettie pushed back Sophie's loose hairs from her face.

"You look just like your *mudder* when she was your age."

"Why didn't you tell me when I met you yesterday?"

"I knew it was you the minute I saw you, but I promised your *vadder* I wouldn't overwhelm you with your past when you couldn't remember on your own!" she said with a half-cry, half-laugh. "I'm your *Aenti* Lettie."

Sophie's face lit up, and her smile widened. She let out a nervous chuckle.

"Are you really my aunt?"

"*Jah,*" Lettie said, pulling Sophie into another hug. "It's so *gut* to be able to tell you that. You don't know how badly I wanted to tell you yesterday."

"It was probably better that you saved it for now," Sophie said. "It probably would have been too much too soon if you'd have said it yesterday, so don't worry about it."

Lettie released her and looked at her soberly. "Are you running from something?"

"I'd like to go into town, I guess," she said. "Simon is mad at me."

"Are you planning on leaving the community?"

Sophie shrugged; she didn't know where she belonged right now.

"I wish you wouldn't leave when we only just found each other again," Lettie said, sniffling. "I had no idea where Hugh moved to; we didn't have a phone then, and he didn't keep in touch the way he said he would. I'm so sorry about that."

"I am too." Sophie lowered her gaze. "I was supposed to stay with Simon and the girls on my old farm, but I'm thinking of going back home; I don't think I belong here."

"If you don't mind me asking; did you run out on your wedding?"

Sophie let a strained chuckle escape her lips. "No! Why would you ask that?"

"Because I think that's the prettiest wedding dress I've seen in the community; I should know because *mei* Becca made it."

Sophie felt her blood run cold. "Did you say *wedding dress?*"

"*Jah.* I would recognize *mei* Becca's wedding dress anywhere.*"

Sophie covered her face with her hands and shook her head. "I'm so sorry," she said, her voice breaking. "I shouldn't have put it on; no wonder Simon was so upset with me! I have to go back and apologize to him; he must have panicked when he saw me in the dress Becca married him in."

"Simon is a *gut mann*—he loved Becca very much. It nearly killed him when she died. I would say his reaction was normal for what he's been through. But if you care for him the way I think you do, trust him; he'd make you a *gut* husband."

Sophie felt her cheeks flush. "I've made a big mess of things with him while I've been staying with him to take care of the girls—your granddaughters. Why didn't he ask *you* to take care of them?"

"I don't see as well as I used to, and my heart isn't what it used to be. I helped as much as I could before you came here, but they wore me out. I had no idea the *Englisher* he'd hired was you, or I'd have been over there your first day."

Sophie smiled. It was wonderful to have an aunt and an uncle—who just happened to be the girl's grandparents.

She looked down at the blue dress. "I got it from the attic; Selma had told me to go up there and get one, but I had no idea this was her wedding dress. I should have picked one of the plain brown work dresses instead of this one, but I couldn't help myself because it is so pretty."

"It's a pretty dress," the woman agreed. "Becca would not have minded you wearing it. She looked so lovely in that dress the day she married Simon."

Sophie sighed. "I feel so bad."

Lettie smiled at her. "I have something that might help."

"What is it?" Sophie asked, feeling giddy.

"I have your *mudder's* cedar trunk full of memories. Your *vadder* gave it to me for safe-keeping. There's a couple of her old dresses in the trunk, and I'm sure they'll fit you; she was petite like you."

"A new dress would be wonderful— especially one of my mother's dresses. I asked my father a million times if he had anything of hers that he could give me to help me remember, but he said he had nothing."

"Do you know why you can't remember?" Lettie asked, caution in her tone.

She had that look in her eye that she knew something Sophie didn't know.

"It was the accident; you were thrown from the buggy and suffered a head injury. You were knocked out, and when you woke up, your memory was gone—all of it. Your *vadder* took you away from here to take you to the best doctors and specialists in the city. The doctors told him you would be in therapy for years."

Sophie cocked her head to one side and wrinkled her brow. "I don't think I got knocked out right away because I had a memory of my mom laying on the street and Charlie horse whinnying. I remembered thinking Charlie was dying but my mother was already gone, and then I don't remember anything else. I don't even seem to have any memories of my childhood except the red barn and picking lilacs for her that grew beside the porch."

Lettie smiled at her, tears rolling down her cheeks. "You poor girl; the doctors said you might never regain any memory from before the accident, but I'm happy to hear he was wrong. Perhaps in time, you will remember more."

Sophie sighed. "It would probably help if my father would have told me *anything* about her while I was growing up. He cheated me out of knowing my family and didn't even tell me I was part Amish."

"Don't be so hard on your *vadder;* he did what he did to protect you. The doctors all told him that it might be too devastating for you to remember and it could stifle your therapy. After the accident, you were like a little *boppli*-baby again. You couldn't talk or walk, and you had to start over again. You lost the first five years of your life."

Sophie burst into uncontrollable sobs. She had no idea what her father had done to protect her. She'd been so angry with him for keeping something from her when it was for her own good. It scared her to think about losing five years of her life to memory loss. "The memories must be in there somewhere," she blubbered. "I had some glimpses of them—but only since I was at Simon's house. I have to go back; I have to remember—even if Simon doesn't want me there."

She sniffled and shuddered from the tears. "I have to tell Simon I'm sorry for taking his wife's wedding dress, and I have to tell my father I'm sorry for getting so mad at him for doing what he thought was best for me."

"Where would you like to go first?" Lettie asked. "I'd love for you to meet the rest of your family, but I'd like to give you the cedar trunk; it's rightfully yours."

A sob escaped her again, but she suppressed it. "I would like to have my mother's things."

"Have you decided to stay in the community?"

Sophie let her gaze drop. "I'm not sure if Simon will let me come back to his house— but—I love him and the girls—and his mother."

She had to say it out loud to someone; why not to her new aunt?

"This is all so overwhelming," Sophie said. "I don't know what I'm doing anymore."

"You're *wilkum* to stay at *mei haus; mei kinner*—your cousins, are all grown up and living on their own now. You could take one of their old rooms if things don't work out with

Simon; he's a *gut mann,* but he might just need a little time. "

"I'd like to stay with you—if it doesn't work out with Simon," she said. "Thank you for the offer. I think I'd like to stay in the community for a while at least. My father was making me stay the entire summer to help Simon. He still needs help, and now that I know the girls are my cousins, I'm committed to helping them."

"You have a *gut* heart—like your *mudder,"* Lettie said. "And it amazes me how much you look like her; she was a beautiful young woman."

"I'm happy that I look like her," Sophie said. "I think I'd like to take a look at what's in my mother's cedar trunk, now if that's alright."

Sophie was eager to get to know her aunt who happened to live only a short distance from her old house, but right now, all she wanted was something bigger than a glimpse of her mother. Simon would keep; perhaps he needed a little bit of time to miss her before he would be ready to listen to her apology.

CHAPTER FIFTEEN

Simon headed back home after seeing Sophie walking toward the Beiler's house. They were good solid people, and she would be safe with them, but he worried they would take Sophie into town where she would likely call her father and ask him to take her home. He wished he would have gotten the man's address so he would know where to reach Sophie. That is if she'd ever speak to him again after the way he'd acted about the dress. Why had he overreacted? It was only a dress and Becca would never wear it again; why couldn't Sophie wear it? Truthfully, Simon thought she looked beautiful in it—almost like a summer bride.

He unhitched the buggy, weary of how he was going to break the news to the girls about Sophie; they were so worried about her already, and they were happy when he decided to go after her. How could he face them knowing how he'd failed them?

Lord, please bring Sophie back to me if it is your will. I love her and didn't get the chance to tell her. Please forgive me for the way I treated her and put forgiveness in her heart for me; I don't want to add to her hurt because she's been through so much.

Sophie met her Uncle Amos, who was too eager to bring the cedar trunk down from their attic for her to go through it. She jiggled her leg as she sat in the front room waiting for the cookies and tea that Lettie was busy putting together in the kitchen, and for the cedar chest to be brought down from the attic.

She could hardly contain herself; she was finally going to see something that belonged to her mother. Her heart raced with excitement; would she recognize any of it? She bolted up from the chair when her aunt entered the room with a tray full of things. "Let me take that for you," she said, taking the tray from the woman.

She'd no more had a chance to take a sip of the tea than her uncle came bounding down the stairs, the wood creaking under the weight.

He sounded strained—as though the trunk was heavy, and she could see when he set it down with a little bit of trouble that it must be.

Sophie collapsed onto the floor and sat before the chest; she ran a hand over it, smiling. This was better than Christmas.

"Go ahead and open it," Lettie said. "I'll sit in the chair and watch; I'm too old to get down on that floor with you."

Sophie put her hands together and paused, a mixture of emotions consuming her. "I'm too excited!" she squealed.

Drawing in a deep breath, she placed her hands on the lid and opened it slowly. She bent to smell the inside of the cedar chest and closed her eyes. "It smells like her!" she said, her lower lip quivering. "I remember she made soap with honeysuckle and oatmeal."

"*Jah,* she did," Lettie said with a sniffle.

Sophie opened her eyes and began to sift through the contents. There were a couple of dresses—pretty ones. One was a deep lavender, one was yellow, and the other one was blue. It was similar to the one she was wearing, but it had a fluted collar, and the organdy apron was attached. The blue was a deeper blue. Sophie lifted the matching organdy prayer *kapp* from the trunk and held it to her cheek. She closed her eyes and smiled, tears dripping down her face.

"Was this her wedding dress?" Sophie asked.

"*Jah,* she was so happy that day, but not as happy as the day you were born."

Sophie looked up at Lettie, her lower lip quivering.

"There are some of your clothes in the bottom—from when you were born. And a couple of pictures your father took."

Sophie dug eagerly to the bottom of the trunk, and there they were; the pictures of her mother.

She held them up and stared into the face, feeling a connection to her. "I look almost identical to her!" She held up one of the pictures. "Who took this one? My father looks so young there—and he's smiling!"

"I took the picture for them," Lettie said. "Pictures are forbidden among the Amish, but she was taking her *rumspringa*—that is when the youth get a taste of the *English* world and make the decision to stay and join the church or leave."

"I read about that online before I came here," Sophie said. "I guess she decided not to join."

"*Jah,* she met your *vadder* during her *rumspringa,* and she married him a week later; they were so in love. It broke your father in two when she died."

"I've never seen that smile on him before," Sophie said. "He must have really loved her; he misses her still so much that he chokes up any time I mention her. I thought that was why he wouldn't talk about her to me."

"He did it to protect you," Lettie said. "The doctors told him if you remember too soon it could hurt you more than help."

"I guess he thought I was ready since he sent me here. I wish I could call him."

"We have a phone," Lettie said. "We live as Mennonite; we still have a buggy, but we have electricity and a phone too."

"Would you mind if I called him?" Sophie asked. "I think I need him to come and visit me so we can talk. I'm not sure if I'll have him take me home, but that depends on Simon. I still need to talk to my dad whether I stay here or not, but I think he needs to know what's going on."

"Whenever you're ready, let me know, and I'll have Amos put the trunk in the buggy so you can take it back with you to share with Simon."

Sophie smiled, thinking about sharing her past with the man she loved. Even if he didn't return her feelings, she'd like to be his friend. She dug through the rest of the contents of the cedar chest, savoring each item.

"May I try on this dress?" she asked, holding up the lavender one.

Lettie nodded. "Of course you can; this stuff belongs to you now."

She showed her to a small bathroom off the kitchen, and Sophie carefully slipped out of Becca's dress and folded it neatly before laying it on the counter. Then she pulled her mother's dress over her head and smoothed it out, admiring the fit in the large bathroom mirror. It was beautiful, but more than that, it felt like coming home as she admired the dress and she couldn't stop smiling. There had been a bar of her mother's homemade soap that had mixed in with her dresses, and it made them smell just like Sophie remembered her.

Simon rushed out of the barn when he heard buggy wheels and a horse coming up his driveway. He smiled with relief when he saw that it was Sophie with Lettie and Amos.

She hopped down from the buggy and bounced on her heels until he closed the space between them. "I found out that they are my Aunt and Uncle!" she squealed. "She's my mother's sister, and she gave me a trunk full of her things, including this dress!"

"It's a fine dress!" he said with a smile.

She reached into the buggy and grabbed Becca's dress from the bench seat and handed it to Simon.

"I'm sorry," Simon said quietly. "I lost my head when I saw you in that dress; it was Becca's wedding dress."

"I'm sorry; I didn't know," Sophie said. "I should have asked if it was alright for me to wear her things. I should have thought about how you would feel seeing me in her wedding dress, but I honestly didn't know it was her wedding dress until Aunt Lettie told me."

"I forgot that you didn't grow up Amish, so you had no way of knowing about the dress."

Sophie smiled at him. "My father is coming in the morning; we have a lot to talk about, but I wanted to talk to you too. If you want me to go, I understand; Aunt Lettie said I could stay with her."

Simon shook his head. "I think the girls would be disappointed if you didn't stay; they've been so worried about you. I was too, except that when I hitched up the buggy to go after you, I saw that you went toward their place, so I decided to give you some time."

She looked at him with yearning in her eyes. "You went after me?"

He nodded. "I'd like you to stay."

She looked up at her aunt and uncle who were patiently waiting for her to make up her mind. "I'm going to stay here; will you please come over and visit with me?"

"We can come over Sunday afternoon if that's alright."

Sophie giggled. "I'll fry up some chicken and make potato salad, and we'll have a picnic out in the yard under the big oak tree!"

"I'll bring a *snitz* pie; it was your *mudder's* favorite," Lettie said.

"I can't wait to try it!" Sophie said with a smile. "Thank you for everything."

She turned to Simon. "Can you get my trunk out of the back of the buggy?"

He looked at her lovingly. "You brought it back with you?"

"Aunt Lettie gave the trunk to me, and I can't wait to share it with you!" she said, excitement in her tone.

He set Becca's wedding dress on top of the trunk and pulled it out from the back of the buggy; he said his goodbyes and took it into the house while Sophie hugged her aunt and uncle one last time before they left. He was glad Sophie was home and couldn't wait for the girls to see she'd returned. He was eager to talk with her, and he planned to do just that after the girls went to bed.

Sophie was met at the kitchen door by two bouncing little girls who threw themselves into her arms. "We're so glad you're back home!" they squealed.

Home; that has a nice ring to it. Lord, please let me stay here. This is my home— where I belong.

"I was so afraid when you left," Katie sniffled. "I didn't think you were coming back."

Sophie crouched down on her haunches to be at eye-level with them. "I'm sorry; I made a mistake. Sometimes grownups make mistakes, and I made a big one."

"Like wearing *Mamm's* wedding dress?" Ellie asked with an innocence that broke Sophie's heart.

"Yes," she admitted. "I'm sorry because I didn't know it was her wedding dress, and that should be saved for the two of you someday when you get married."

"We forgive you," they said.

Sophie's lower lip quivered as she pulled them into another hug. "I love you both."

"We love you too!" they both said.

Simon entered the room just then after putting the cedar trunk in his room for her. "I'd like to talk with you after the girls go to bed tonight."

She nodded. "Okay."

"What are we making for supper?" Ellie asked.

"If you picked the vegetables, we could make a salad, and I think your *mammi* said something about teaching me to make meatloaf."

Selma entered the room just then looking sleepy. She imagined all the drama had probably worn the woman out and she'd taken an extra long nap.

"It's *gut* to see you're back," Selma said with a smile that seemed a little less crooked than yesterday. "I hope you have a *gut* story for me."

"I do! Lettie is my mother's sister; sit down at the table, and I'll tell you all about it in between you teaching me how to make meatloaf."

Simon sat on the porch swing next to Sophie, the warmth of her leg touching his sending sparks of excitement all the way to his toes. She pushed lightly, the squeak of the chain masking the awkward silence between them.

"I wanted to apologize again for the way I reacted today," he said. "I wish I could take my words back, but I can't so I pray you'll forgive me."

"I forgive you," she said. "I'd like you to forgive me too; I overstepped my boundaries, and I'm so sorry."

He smiled and patted her hand. "I forgive you, and it's forgotten."

"Now that we got that out of the way, I need to tell you why my father is coming tomorrow."

Simon felt his heart lurch. "You're leaving?"

"No, I plan on staying, but there are some things I need to clear up with my father—mostly stuff about my mother and the accident."

"He's coming for a long visit, then?"

She nodded. "Is that alright?"

"*Jah;* he's *wilkum* to stay with you in the main *haus.*"

"I doubt he will stay overnight; if he does, he'll take a room in town. But that doesn't matter. I need to clear the air with him; we didn't part ways on good terms, and I'd like to fix that."

219

"I'm happy to hear you plan to stay; I'll admit I was worried you would be leaving. I'd like you to consider staying beyond the summer."

"I'm sure I could stay with my aunt," she said.

Simon blew out a long breath; she was not going to make this easy for him. "That's not what I had in mind; I'd like to take you for a buggy ride."

"Is that Amish *code* for dating?" she asked with a giggle.

He chuckled. "*Jah,* I suppose it is, but I feel a little too old to be dating."

"I'd like to take a buggy ride with you," she said. "And I don't think you could ever be too old to take a buggy ride."

"This is true. *Ach,* I was so worried when you left that I was never going to see you again," Simon said. "I've been so stubborn and was trying too hard not to allow myself to feel the way I do, but I can't help myself; I love you, Sophie."

He pressed his lips against hers, and she put her arms around his neck and deepened the kiss.

"I love you too," she whispered.

He kissed her again, pulling her so close it was almost indecent, but he couldn't help himself. He wanted her for his wife.

"Will you marry me?" he blurted out.

"Do I still get a buggy ride?" she asked with a giggle.

"*Jah,* we can take all the buggy rides you want to for the rest of our lives; please say you'll marry me."

She smiled and nodded. "Yes!"

His mouth found hers again; her breaths moaning as she leaned into the kiss. He felt safe with her. She loved him; he could feel it in her embrace and her kiss.

Sophie rolled over in Simon's bed and hugged his shirt, pulling it close and breathing

221

it in. Her father would be here before noon, and she had much to do to prepare for his visit, but she couldn't stop thinking about Simon's proposal. She loved him more than she ever thought she could love another person. He made her feel safe and loved. Would her father give his consent to marry Simon? Not that she needed his permission, but Simon was an honorable man and stated he intended to ask her father for her hand in marriage. She thought it was sweet and old-fashioned, but sweet.

She smiled thinking of their kiss. Simon was a good kisser, but the love between them would have made even a bad kiss a good one.

She couldn't wait to tell the girls she was going to be their new mom; she and Simon had agreed they would tell them together in the morning before their soon-to-be grandpa showed up. She was excited about her visit with her dad; she couldn't wait to share with him all the things she'd learned since she'd been here. He would certainly be surprised to taste her cooking, but she prayed he wouldn't get upset seeing her in her mother's dresses.

Sophie ran out to greet her dad when he pulled into the driveway. She threw herself into his arms the moment he got out of the car.

"It's so good to see you; I've missed you," she said with a giggle.

"It's good to see you so happy; I was afraid when I got here, you'd be packed and jumping in the car and begging me to take you home."

She giggled; he had no idea how close she came to doing that very thing yesterday. But today was a new day; it was the start of a whole new life, and she wanted her dad to be a part of it.

"I met mom's sister!" she blurted out. "I'm so happy you sent me here. I don't ever want to leave."

"Simon might not agree with that," Hugh said, concern in his eyes. "Maybe you could come back to visit."

She stood in front of him and looked sincerely into his eyes. "No, Dad, I mean I'm staying here—with Simon and the girls."

He scrunched his brow. "Did something happen to his mother? Did she get worse?"

She shook her head. "I don't think you understand, Dad."

Simon came up behind her and touched her elbow. "What she means is that I've asked Sophie to marry me, and I'd like your permission."

Hugh looked at his daughter soberly. "You don't want a marriage in name only, Sophie; you're too young for that."

"No, Dad; you don't understand," she said. "I love Simon."

His eyes widened. "That was fast!"

"Aunt Lettie told me you and mom got married a week after you met, so six days is not too fast," Sophie said, hoping the mention of her mother wouldn't upset him.

He nodded, becoming misty-eyed. "Yes, we did do that; I loved that woman more than my own life."

"I feel the same way about Simon."

His eyes brightened. "Then you have my blessing."

"Thank you, Dad," Sophie squealed.

Simon shook his hand, and the two of them walked off toward the barn. She assumed it was so her father could have a talk with Simon. She wasn't worried; should she be?

Sophie sat across from her father on the porch; Simon had taken the girls in town to get ice cream to give the two of them some time to talk.

"I'm sorry I didn't let you visit here sooner," Hugh said. "I thought spoiling you would keep you from the hurt that awaited you here."

"You didn't spoil me, Dad" Sophie admitted. "You were only trying to protect me."

"I was afraid that if you remembered too much, it would take away that sparkle in your eye that took so long to return after the accident. I'm sorry I denied you your heritage; your mother would be happy you've come back—and that you'll be living in our old house."

"It's comforting to know she sat on this very porch once—full of dreams for her future," Sophie said. "I realize that we may only have the moment that we're in, and we should always strive to make each moment count for something. I'm sorry for the way I spoke to you the last time we were together— and for the way I acted. Being around Simon has given me a new understanding for your grief; I pray that I never have to experience that kind of grief."

"Tomorrow I'd like to go visit her grave," Hugh said. "Would you like to go with me?"

Sophie smiled and nodded, feeling relief that her father was finally ready to share her mother with her.

Sophie stood in front of the long mirror Aunt Lettie had brought over for her so she could see how she looked in her mother's wedding dress. She smiled thinking of how her mother must have felt on her wedding day. It turned out that the dress had belonged to her cousin, who had changed her mind about marrying her betrothed and so her mother had worn the dress instead when she'd married Sophie's father.

She looked in the mirror again not caring that her mother hadn't made the dress; it was special to her for the sole reason she'd worn it on her special day.

A knock at the door brought Sophie back to the present. "Come in," she said.

Her father poked his head in the door and smiled. "You look beautiful—just like your mother."

"Thank you, Dad."

"Are you ready to go marry Simon?"

"I am; I love him so much. I can't wait."

Hugh chuckled. "You have an Amish heart—like your mother."

Sophie hugged her father once more, and then he walked her toward the trellis behind her old, new house where Simon and the girls waited to become her husband and daughters.

Jah, it is gut to be Amish, she thought with a giggle.

THE END

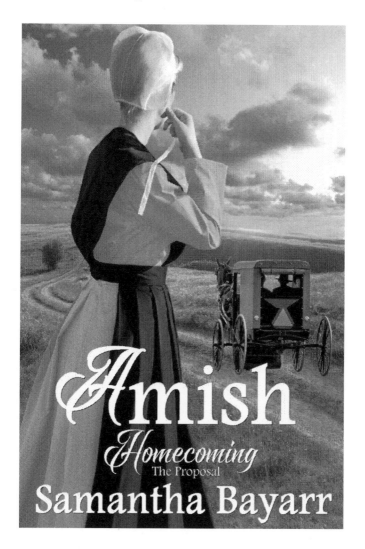

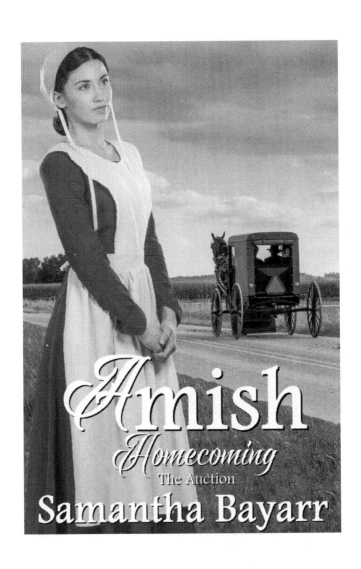

Amish
Homecoming
The Auction

Samantha Bayarr

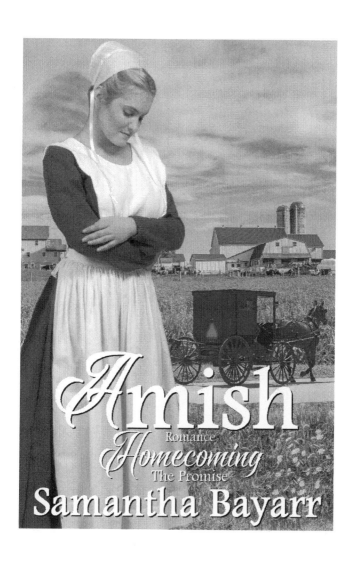

Amish
Romance
Homecoming
The Promise
Samantha Bayarr

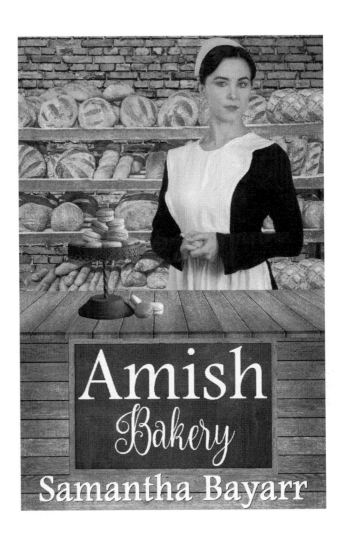

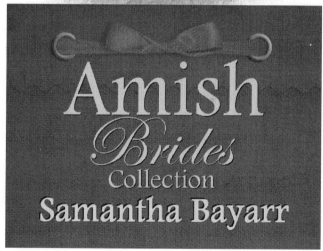

Amish
Brides
Collection
Samantha Bayarr

233

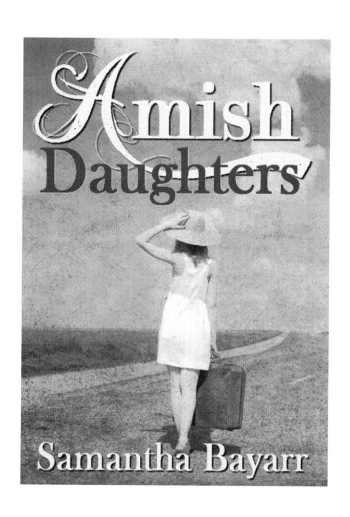

Made in the USA
Middletown, DE
20 April 2019